Fringed Privilege

Derrick Frank

Knighten Truce Global, LLC
Maryland

Fringed Privilege

by Derrick Frank

Published 2025 by Knighten Truce Global, LLC
Bel Air, Maryland 21014
https://md-knighten-truce-global-llc-yevib.zensmb.com/

First Edition Published by Knighten Truce Global, LLC

Printed in the United States of America

1 2 3 4 5 6 7 8 9 0

ISBN-13: 979-8-9931293-1-0
e-ISBN: 979-8-9931293-0-3

Library of Congress Control Number: 2025920160

Editor: Ayanna Moo-Young

This book is inspired by my children. It is a gift to them — a guide to help them seek joy and purpose by looking inward instead of outward.

Contents

Preface

This story is a modern-day parable, a microcosm of the society we live in today. It is not a tale of individuals, but rather a personification of the qualities within us all: those we embody, those we desire, and those we may already possess but are buried deep inside. It explores how we often fail to find our true purpose and use our talents to pursue desires that are misaligned with our inner nature that ultimately work against us. When we are disconnected from our source, our inner truth, life manifests in ways we cannot fully explain. But when we change the way we see things, the things we see begin to change.

In this story, the sport of lacrosse is amidst the events that unfold. The sport itself symbolizes how something sacred can be transformed, even distorted. What many see today as just a sport was originally a ritual practiced by the Indigenous Peoples of the Americas as a ceremonial game to honor the Creator. The ball represented the soul passed from one person to another, ultimately seeking union with its goal. Over time, this ritual was stripped of its sacred meaning and reshaped into a competitive sport. Therefore, what was once an act of worship and free expression has become exclusive and commercialized, divorced from its original purpose. This transformation mirrors how our own lives can lose direction when we stray from our authentic paths.

This book was born during a time when I struggled to find my way through life. I was doing what seemed acceptable by society's standards; yet I felt like a hamster spinning on a wheel. I felt unhappy, depressed, and stuck. But once I began to question and change the unnatural habits I had accepted as the norm, the world around me shifted, and the truths that I clung onto began to unravel.

I realized this story is not just mine, it is the story of all humanity. It is about the unknown, the fear, and the pain that we experience from chasing things that are not in our blueprint, and how our deepest desires can sometimes become the very cages that hold us captive. Writers often use demons and monsters to symbolize the struggles we face in the world. But the truth is, the real monsters are often our own thoughts and emotions. When we learn to see this, we can become our own heroes. We'll discover that we have the strength to confront the beasts within, to reclaim our power, and to free ourselves from the mental prisons we have built.

Chapter 1: Face-Off

In lacrosse, a face-off is how the game begins—a clash at the center field where two players fight for control. It's raw, quick, and symbolic. Victory doesn't go to the strongest, but to the most focused. Just like life, it's not about who starts with the ball, but who fights hardest to gain possession of their destiny.

"A hundred right hand, then a hundred left hand! Two laps around the track. After that, we'll work the ladder and finish with cone drills. Today's a light day," bellowed a large, burly man from across the turf field.

Dillion, small and sure-handed, gripped his lacrosse stick tightly. The oversized stick seemed nearly too big for his six-year-old frame.

"I'm tired, Dad. Can I just do fifty catches and then run the track?" Dillion sighed, his voice edged with exhaustion.

"In order to be the best, you've got to train harder than everyone, especially when no one's watching," his father replied, dismissing Dillion's slouched shoulders with a wave of command.

"But I'm six! I should be playing video games or riding my bike right now!" Dillion protested, his eyes searching his father's face for a sliver of leniency.

His father crouched down, softened his voice, and said with a grin, "The kids watching YouTube sit on the bench. If you want to be a gamer, that's fine. But if you want to be *great* at anything, you've got to work hard, train smart, and be consistent. Those are the keys to life. You *love* lacrosse, remember? I'm just here to keep you focused."

The evening grew stale and thick as the sun dipped low. Sweat poured down Dillion's forehead like water rolling off the back of an Olympic swimmer. He pushed through the last lap, his feet pounded the track in small, determined steps.

"Okay, that's enough. Let's pack up," his father called out, as Dillion stretched toward an imaginary finish line he'd created in his mind to symbolize the end of the grind.

"No cone drills tonight. Your mom's got dinner ready, and you've still got homework," his father added.

Dillion bent over, panting heavily, his frame trembling. He gasped for air as though he had just emerged from fifty leagues beneath the sea.

"And," his father said, leaning close and gently wrapping his arm around Dillion's shoulders, "you owe me three chapters and a book report."

The two walked back to their cherry red SUV, the trunk filled with cones, ladders, and a bucket of scuffed lacrosse balls. As his father packed the gear, a memory flickered—his own childhood in West Baltimore. Back then, there were no fields to play on, and his father wasn't around to guide him. He went home after school to four walls and silence. He had sworn that if he ever had kids, he would push them toward greatness, no matter what it took.

Looking at Dillion, small and strong in his own way, he felt that vow reaffirmed. He knew his son had something special, something bright.

Before pulling out of the lot, he offered a final piece of wisdom, knowing his son was too tired to argue back: "To achieve greatness, stay diligent in your craft, whatever that may be. If you want to be a doctor, study anatomy and learn how to heal. If you want to be a janitor, learn to shine a floor better than anyone else. Whatever you do, do it well. Be excellent. Be consistent."

He gave Dillion a gentle pat on the head, and the SUV hummed to life as he started the ignition and drove home.

Back at the house, after unloading gear, Dillion was greeted by his mother's warm embrace.

"You hungry?" she asked. "Your teacher emailed me. She said your project was a hit with the class today. She's really impressed."

"It was okay," Dillion mumbled, dragging his bookbag upstairs.

Dillion was a bright student: self-motivated, intuitive, focused. A prodigy in the making. But like all gifted kids, he needed loving hands to shape his energy. Without direction, he could easily fall into thinking he already knew enough.

Downstairs, his mother set the table as she did every night. "Meatloaf, mashed potatoes, and green beans," she called out.

Dillion and his father emerged from their showers and joined her. She placed wooden serving bowls on the table with the care of a set designer staging a home for a lifestyle magazine. Presentation always mattered to her.

As the three sat in peaceful silence, she reached for the bowl of potatoes and asked gently, "How was work?"

"Long, but good," her husband replied through a mouthful of meatloaf, swallowing before offering a fuller response.

He was a crime scene investigator. But he never talked about his work at the dinner table. He believed that everything had its place, and death, crime, and trauma had no place in the sanctuary of family.

He didn't want Dillion curious about the darkness he dealt with daily. He saw something in his son—something limitless—and it was his duty to guide him toward the light.

After dinner, Dillion knew what was expected of him: three chapters, a book report, prayers, and sleep. That was the nightly order of business, no exceptions. His father believed in routine, structure, and discipline.

"You ready for bed yet?" his father asked, peeking into Dillion's bedroom.

"Yeah, just finished saying my prayers," Dillion replied, rising from his knees. He unfolded the covers and slipped between the lukewarm sheets, the cotton hugging him like a familiar friend.

"Dad, can I ask you a question?" Dillion squeaked, peering out from beneath the blanket.

"What's that, son?" his father answered, leaning against the doorframe.

"What would happen if you and Mom didn't want to be together anymore?"

His father blinked, momentarily caught off guard. "Where'd that come from?" he asked, surprised but calm.

"I just wanted to know ... because it's a thing, right? Mommies and daddies leave each other sometimes?"

His father walked over and sat on the edge of the bed. "That's not a thing for us—not now, not ever. So don't worry about that. You just focus on school, your grades, and being a kid."

He gently laid a hand on Dillion's forehead and kissed the top of his head. "Get some rest. I've got to work some overtime tonight."

The next morning, Dillion awoke the same way he did most days, to the soft chirping of birds in the tree just outside his window. He rolled out of bed and padded to his parents' room. The drapes were drawn tight, keeping even the boldest rays of morning light at bay.

He peeked inside. His mother was curled up beneath the lavender comforter, barely visible in the shadows of the room.

"Mom?" he whispered. "Can I walk to school today?"

She stirred, lifting her head slightly. "You know I don't think you're quite ready to walk by yourself yet," she said sleepily, then buried her face back into the warmth of her pillow.

"But Dad would let me!" Dillion protested. "I'm turning seven next month! And school's just down the street! Dad said the reason we moved here is because it's safe."

She slowly turned to face him, voice firm but kind. "I'll be up in a minute to make you breakfast and take you to school. I feel better knowing you're there safe and sound. This isn't about you, it's about *my* peace of mind."

She held his gaze a moment longer, making sure her reasoning landed. She knew if she didn't explain herself now, the debate would stretch until one of them gave in, and it wasn't going to be her.

"Okay, Mom," Dillion sighed, conceding. He shut the door softly and headed downstairs to gather his homework and the book report he had to turn in.

"What do you want to eat—dippy eggs, cereal, or a honey bun?" his mother called out, retightening the robe around her waist as she descended the dark staircase into the living room.

She always asked, but she already knew the answer.

"Dippy eggs," Dillion mumbled with a sleepy smile.

He wolfed down his breakfast, quick and focused, as he always did, then grabbed his books for school.

As they loaded into the car for the short ride to school, Dillion mentally braced himself for the usual routine, predicable day.

When he arrived, the morning unfolded like any other. The bell rang. The class settled. Everyone slid into their familiar spots. Dillion took his seat next to Jason just like he had every day since school started.

"So, what do you think is better, lacrosse or football?" Jason asked, turning toward him.

"Huh? What?" Dillion replied, caught off guard.

"Who even plays lacrosse?" Jason muttered. "I mean, only white boys play lacrosse."

Dillion stared at him, confused by the sudden commentary.

Jason wasn't finished. "What are you, anyway?" He asked, like it was the first time they'd ever spoken.

"I'm … half and half," Dillion answered, unsure why he even had to.

Jason looked him over like he was trying to find something new. "Well, you look White but act Black. You should play football or basketball, not some weird sport no one plays. Like, who's even famous for that? You got a Jordan? A Kobe?"

Dillion blinked.

He had never thought about himself that way before. He'd never had to. In his neighborhood, everyone was different, and no one seemed to care. He had friends of every shade and shape, and all that mattered was who you were.

Now, sitting at his desk with his Johns Hopkins Lacrosse shooter shirt and his blue basketball shoes, Dillion felt a strange tug in his chest. Why *shouldn't* he love lacrosse?

He thought quickly. "Paul Rabil. Kyle Harrison. Lyle Thompson. Dave Pietramala," he said in a firm whisper.

Jason rolled his eyes, but before anything else could be said—

"DILLION CARTER!" The teacher snapped from the front of the classroom.

He jerked out of his thoughts. "Present!" he shouted, cheeks flushed.

"Dillion," the teacher continued, eyebrow raised, "are you with us today? When I take attendance, it would be nice if you'd at least pretend to be here."

"Yes, ma'am," Dillion murmured, trying to ignore the stares now pointed in his direction.

A soft voice floated over his shoulder. "You okay?"

Dillion turned around and saw Malia. One of the few kids in his neighborhood who really knew him. Their moms were friends. She had once spent afternoons at his house, eating snacks and watching cartoons while their parents worked late.

Her presence was comforting, like finding solid ground in a room that suddenly felt tilted.

"Is Jason messing with you again? He's weird," Malia said, narrowing her eyes at the back of Jason's head as he doodled footballs arcing over crooked goalposts.

"Nah, I'm good," Dillion replied softly, trying not to draw the teacher's attention as she continued roll call.

"You getting a ride from my mom today?" Dillion asked, glancing over his shoulder.

"Yeah," Malia said. "She called your mom this morning. That's why I was late, she had to get ready for work."

The school day continued as usual, and when the final bell rang, Dillion lined up outside with the other car riders, scanning the crowd for his mom's red Chevy.

"Dillion! Hey, wait up!" Malia's voice rang out behind him just as he stepped off the curb.

Dillion turned to see her jogging toward him, her massive book bag bouncing with every step.

"Did you forget I was riding with you today?" she puffed, catching her breath.

"Nah, I knew you'd catch up. You always do."

They hopped into the car just as Dillion's mom turned to greet them.

"How was school?" she asked, as Malia struggled to shut the door, her book bag wedged awkwardly in the frame.

"Great!" Malia grinned, finally settling in.

Before the car could pull away, Dillion's mom grabbed her Nikon from the passenger seat.

"Aww, you guys look so cute. Let me get a picture!"

"Mom!" Dillion groaned, sinking into the seat. "You're holding up the line! Everyone's staring!"

"You're only this age once," she said as the camera flash popped in their faces.

"There; harmless," she smiled, tucking the camera away and gently easing the car forward like nothing had happened.

Malia smirked. "So … what was Jason saying to you today?"

"Nothing," Dillion muttered.

"It had to be something. The teacher called your name like three times before you even blinked," Malia said, nudging him.

"Mom," Dillion said suddenly, "What am I? Am I half and half? Black or White?"

His mother's eyes shifted to the rearview mirror. Both hands stayed steady at 12 and 2 on the steering wheel.

"Where did that come from?" she asked, voice calm but alert.

"Well, Jason made it seem like the only way I could play lacrosse was if I was White," Dillion said. "He said I 'act Black but dress white'."

Dillion's mother turned her eyes from the rearview mirror and focused on the road.

"Well ... you're *you,*" she said gently. "Unique and special. You're not defined by color." she nodded to herself, proud of the answer.

"My mother was adopted. Her maiden name is Sanchez. We don't know a lot more than that; she was adopted in California. My father met her while he was in the military and stationed out there. He's from Western Maryland. They're about as plain as vanilla."

"So, I'm not Black then?" Dillion asked firmly.

"Do you *not* want to be Black?" Malia cut in from the back seat. "I'm Black."

"I'm just saying, I'm lighter than all the Black kids, but my hair isn't straight like the white kids. And I play lacrosse."

"Dillion, people are different. Black, white, blue or purple," his mother said, her voice softening, trying to steer things to safety.

"But I'm not purple," Dillion muttered. "I've never seen a purple person."

His mother smiled slightly but said nothing as they pulled into the carport, the teal siding of the house catching the last of the evening light.

"I think this is a conversation for your dad," she said, getting out of the car, stage-left from a conversation teetering on the edge of something deeper.

It was 8:05 p.m. when Dillion's father arrived home. The house was dimly lit and warm. He kicked off his shoes at the door and headed into the kitchen, where Monday night's leftovers were waiting. Taco night. Even better, the tacos were pre-made.

He hovered over them, debating–cold, microwave, or oven. He settled on the oven, not wanting the lettuce to wilt too much. As he placed them neatly on a tray, the stairwell light flicked on behind him.

"Dad?" he recognized Dillion's voice.

"What's up, buddy? How was school?"

"It was cool. Can I ask you a question?"

"Does it involve girls?" his dad grinned.

"No," Dillion said flatly.

"Then sure. Just lemme pop these tacos in real quick."

He slid the tray into the oven and turned the heat to low. Then he turned to his son.

"What's on your mind?"

"What am I, Dad?"

His father paused. "What do you mean?"

"Am I Black?" Dillion asked.

"You're more yellow than anything," his father replied with a chuckle, eyeing Dillion's beige skin and sandy brown hair. He laughed lightly, but behind his smile, he paused. He had always planned to have this talk one day, just not after a ten-hour shift.

“You’re mixed, son. Your mother’s White; I’m Black, or African American if we’re being formal. Race … it’s complicated. But in America, when you're mixed, you're usually considered Black.”

“So, I shouldn’t be playing lacrosse then?”

“Why not?” his father asked as he pulled the now-overheated tacos from the oven.

“Because Black people don’t play lacrosse.”

“Son,” his father said, setting the tray down with a sigh, “people can play whatever they want. Race doesn’t determine what you can or can’t do. That’s just noise.”

He looked at his son, who now stared at the wall like it might offer some sort of answer.

“You’re not defined by a color. You’re defined by the choices you make. Just be you. Follow your heart. Don’t get stuck on small things in life. The color of your skin, while important, isn’t what makes you who you are. A lot of people never learn that.”

He picked up his glass of water, took a sip, and then set it down firmly. The water swirled in the glass, catching Dillion’s eye.

“To be honest,” his father continued, “I only recently started learning about our family’s history—on my side, at least. My grandmother Carol: she lives in Port Arthur, Texas. She told me her grandfather was from Oklahoma, part of the Choctaw Nation. He took the railroad south to Washington, Louisiana, and eventually settled there.”

Dillion listened, his head tilted, curiosity growing.

“And on my mother’s side, her grandfather—your great-great-great-grandfather — was an indentured servant from England. His name was Alan Hill. He settled in Stafford, Virginia, and married a Black woman who, we believe, was part Blackfoot Native American.”

“Really?” Dillion asked, eyes wide.

“Yeah. I didn’t know any of this until I was grown. Your grandfather’s obituary led me to some names I’d never heard growing up. We’ve got a lot of history in our blood, but none of it changes this simple fact–you still have to be *you*. You still have to be Dillion.”

His father stood and glanced at the microwave clock.

“It’s late. Time for bed; we both have to be up early.”

He picked up one of the now room-temperature tacos, bit into it, and with half a shell hanging from his mouth, gave Dillion a sideways smile. That was his signal: the conversation was over.

The whistle blew, sharp and cold in the morning air. Dillion exploded off the line. The face-off was a blur of motion—plastic on plastic, arms jostling, sticks scraping for possession. For a split second, the ball bounced free. Dillion saw it first.

He lunged, scooping it up cleanly, tucking the shaft of his stick tight to his chest as a Fallston midfielder crashed into his side. Dillion absorbed the contact and spun out, his cleats cutting through wet grass. Cheers erupted from the sideline.

“Go, D!” his dad’s voice echoed across the field.

Dillion sprinted down the right alley, scanning the crease. He saw his attackman, Malik, break toward the net—hand raised, calling for it. Dillion slung a low sidearm pass that skimmed inches above the turf and hit Malik's stick in stride. Malik caught it, turned, and fired.

Goal! The net snapped. The ref threw up both hands.

The Eagles bench erupted. Dillion jogged back toward midfield, bumping gloves with teammates. He looked toward the sideline where his dad stood, arms crossed, giving him a proud nod.

But the celebration was short-lived.

Fallston struck back fast. Their face-off guy was sharp, bigger than Dillion, and won the next draw clean. Their offense worked with machine-like precision. Pass. Cut. Shot. Goal. The score was now tied, 1–1.

The next few possessions were hard-fought. Dillion took a check to the ribs that knocked the wind out of him but held onto the ball. One of his defensemen slipped on a muddy patch, giving up an easy fast-break goal. By halftime, Fallston led 3–2.

Dillion sat on the grass, helmet off, pouring water down his face. He glanced at his teammates. Some were laughing, others quietly looking at their cleats. A few just seemed tired.

He looked at his dad, kneeling in front of the team with a clipboard in one hand.

"Listen up," his father said. "You're in this game. You've made it a fight. Now finish it."

His dad didn't yell. He didn't lecture. He looked right at Dillion and said, "Be the spark. Not the star. Sparks change games."

The second half started fast and physical. Dillion began to feel the rhythm—the ball in his stick, the weight of each pass, the give of the turf beneath his cleats. He dodged past a defender on a sweep, drew the slide, and dumped it down to Malik who scored again. Tied game.

On defense, his team stiffened. Their goalie made two crucial saves. Dillion rode hard after a turnover, stripping the Fallston middie and scooping the ball like it was instinct.

With under a minute left, the game was tied 5–5. Coach called timeout. The plan was simple: get the ball to Dillion. Let him create.

The whistle blew. Dillion took the ball at the top of the box. He juked right, rolled back left, the defender trailing him off balance. He sprinted into space, saw the goalie shift near post—and flicked a behind-the-back shot low and away.

The net rippled. The sideline erupted. 6–5. Eagles.

Dillion took the ball from the ground as swiftly as an eagle skimming the surface of a river, clutching an unsuspecting trout in its talons. He surged forward, eyes scanning the field. No clear pass. The goal revealed itself—the goalie shifting awkwardly, adjusting, then readjusting, uncertain of Dillion's rhythm. Right hand. Switch to left. Back again. Then—*swoop*—the snap of the net as the ball slammed home. A perfect start.

Dillion always played games this way: dominating the faceoff, securing an early goal to give his team a burst of confidence and plant doubt in the minds of their opponents. But then, as usual, his father pulled him out of the game.

"Why did you take me out?" Dillion asked, panting lightly.

"Get a drink," his father said without looking at him.

“I’m not thirsty.”

“Get a breather.”

“I’m not tired.”

This time, Dillion’s father turned his full attention away from the game. His eyes met his son’s, calm but firm. He motioned him aside, away from the kids on the bench watching the exchange with curious eyes.

“Let the other guys play,” he said. “They have to learn how to function without you. They need to develop.”

Dillion clenched his jaw, grabbed the Gatorade his dad had bought earlier, and took a bitter gulp that hit the back of his throat like dry chalk. He stood with the others on the sideline, helmet tucked under his arm, eyes fixed on the field, waiting. But his name was never called.

The final whistle blew. The scoreboard read 6–5. They’d lost.

The team trudged to midfield, dragging their sticks, offering low-effort low fives and muttered “good games” to the other team. Back at the sideline, helmets came off. Cleats stomped clumps of grass from the soles. Bags zipped and shoulder pads unstrapped.

Dillion walked toward his father, his stick hanging at his side.

“Why didn’t you put me back in?” he asked, eyes fixed on the ground.

His father didn’t answer at first.

“Dillion, are you hurt?” his mother asked, stepping away from a group of family friends.

"No," he mumbled. "Dad benched me."

His father turned, slowing his stride. "You have to learn to be coachable," he said flatly. "Just because I'm your dad doesn't mean you get to question me during a game. I won't always be your coach. You need to learn to follow direction, just like everyone else."

His mother gave a quiet sigh. "Did you have to be that extreme?" she asked, her voice low but edged with concern as she saw the glassy shimmer in Dillion's eyes.

"Dillion has to understand that he can't do whatever he wants," his father replied. "There's a structure to all of this. A chain of command. That lesson starts here."

He turned and walked ahead, the gravel crunching beneath his cleats.

Dillion's mother placed her hands on his shoulders. He hunched them up as if every word from his father added weight, like invisible pads being stacked on his back. The walk to the car was quiet, heavy with emotion.

At home, after gear was stowed and cleats were left by the door, Dillion slumped on the couch, still in his practice shorts. His father called to him from the recliner.

"Dillion. Come sit. Let's talk."

"Dillion."

"Yes?"

"I wanted to talk to you briefly about the game. I owe you an apology."

"It's okay, Dad."

His father looked away for a moment, rubbing his hands together.

"I get in my head sometimes," he said. "I just know life isn't always going to be perfect. You're a great kid, but I won't always be there to put you in the game. I needed to see how you handled that."

He sat forward in his chair, speaking gently but firmly.

"I wanted to see if you still cared about the team when you weren't playing. Did you cheer them on? Did you keep your head in the game, even from the sideline? Sometimes that matters more than a goal or a win. That's what builds character."

Dillion looked at his socks, which were once white but now dulled with dirt and asphalt stains.

"I guess I never thought about that being a part of the game too," he said quietly.

His father nodded.

"Maybe I push too hard sometimes. But I'm trying to give you the world the way I've seen it. Life's not fair. But how we handle it, that's what sets us apart."

They embraced without another word. Dillion understood. His father didn't just want him to be a good player; he wanted him to be unbreakable.

Chapter 2: Stickball

Originally played by Native American tribes, "stickball" was more than a sport—it was spiritual, a way to settle disputes, to prepare for war, to bring healing. It was called "The Creator's Game." For Dillion and Malia, stickball—lacrosse—becomes a quiet metaphor for how they learn to navigate a world of fire and silence, of broken homes and dreams barely held together. This isn't just a game. It's survival. And somewhere in the chaos, maybe even redemption.

The next game came fast, and this time, Dillion had a guest—Malia. Her mother was working a double shift at the hospital, and she tagged along with Dillion's family for the day.

"What's so interesting about playing lacrosse every weekend?" Malia asked as the car pulled into the dusty parking lot.

"My dad makes me," Dillion said, watching the field. "He says it's the Creator's game. Native Americans played it to honor God."

Malia rolled her eyes, laughing.

"Is that what your dad told you to say? You sound like a museum tour guide. Looks like boys hitting each other with sticks to me."

Dillion didn't answer. He was focused. Today, it wasn't about convincing anyone. It wasn't even about winning. It was about proving something—maybe even just to himself.

He stepped onto the field like a man on a mission. Eight goals. Seven assists. Countless takeaways. He chased down every loose ball with a ferocity that turned heads. He played like someone who had been forged in the fire of last week's lesson.

His father watched him silently from the sideline, arms crossed, eyes tracking his son's every move. He saw the edge, the focus, the resilience. This was what he'd hoped for, not just talent, but grit. Not just performance, but purpose.

After the game, he met Dillion near the bench.

"Good game, son. You played well. But more importantly, you carried yourself like a leader." He ruffled his son's sweat-soaked faux hawk as they walked off the field.

"I still don't know how the 'Creator' enjoys people beating each other with sticks," Malia joked as she helped gather his gear, "but you were good. I think." She tilted her head, teasing.

"I tried to pay attention, but it was kinda boring. People were yelling your name a lot, though, so that must be a good thing."

Dillion didn't respond, half annoyed, half smiling.

Malia was dropped off at home where she settled in.

"Baby, can you get me the tea off the stove, please?"

Her grandmother's voice came from the darkened back room. Malia was in the next room, playing with her doll when she heard the call. She walked into the kitchen and pushed a stool up to the stove. The teapot hissed steam from its spout. She reached carefully, poured the hot water into a small porcelain cup, and stirred in a spoonful of honey.

"Just honey, right?"

"Yes, baby. Thank you."

Malia tiptoed back into the bedroom. Her grandmother, partially upright in bed, was physically disabled, but her mind was sharp. Malia set the tea on the nightstand.

"Let it cool for a moment, Nana."

Her grandmother gave a tired smile. Malia turned, picked up the bedpan, and walked to the bathroom to flush it. When she returned, her grandmother reached for her hand.

"Anything else, Nana?"

"No, baby. Your mama should be home soon. I hate that you have to do all this. But her new job means these long shifts for a while."

Malia nodded. She didn't complain. This was just life for her. Not fair, but real. And she, like Dillion, was learning how to carry it gracefully and quietly, without letting it crush her.

Malia and her mother had recently left their home after her father, an angry, broken man, had come home drunk again. This time, he was yelling and stumbling as usual and tripped over a pair of shoes left near the doorway. That was enough to spark another one of his violent tirades. He stormed into Malia's room, hurled the shoes at her while she slept, then yanked open her closet, grabbing armfuls of clothes. Without a word, he marched to the backyard, stuffed them into the grill, doused them in lighter fluid, and lit a match.

Malia barely remembered the shouting. What she did remember was the sudden brightness of the flames from her bedroom window and her mother, breathless and terrified, pulling her from bed and rushing her into the back of their old station wagon. They fled in silence and never returned.

Since that night, Malia had been living with her grandmother, her father's mother. The same woman who now lay bedridden in a quiet house on Maple Street. She'd had a minor heart attack a few months earlier. A stent was placed in her chest, and though the surgery saved her life, it had left her legs weak and unreliable. She couldn't walk without help. Still, she never hesitated to take Malia and her mother in.

She blamed herself for the way her son had turned out. For every bruise, every broken promise, every scar he left behind. And because she couldn't fix him, she made it her mission to fix what he destroyed, especially when it came to Malia.

Malia's maternal grandparents were gone, and with her mother working long shifts at the hospital, Nana was all she had.

Their house sat across from a family that seemed perfect. The lawn was trimmed every Saturday; pink roses bloomed perfectly against the hedges. Malia watched them from her bedroom window: the boy and his father, tossing balls, sharing laughs. The mother always had a camera. She captured everything—first steps, backyard cartwheels, even quiet moments like a hug at the mailbox.

Malia wished her father had played with her like that. Instead, he bought her Barbie dolls after hangovers and tantrums, thinking toys would erase the fear. They didn't, but she kept the dolls. They were all she had left from her old home.

One day, she saw the boy riding his bike in circles near the sidewalk. She waited until Nana fell asleep with the TV on and quietly slipped out the front door.

"Hey," she said, standing at the edge of the driveway. "What's your name?"

The boy popped a wheelie in response, then dropped the front tire back to the pavement.

"Uh, Dillion," he replied, surprised. "Who are you? Miss Rose lives there; I've never seen you before."

"That's my Nana. We'll be here for a little bit. I'm starting at Steep Creek on Monday. Do you go there?"

"Yeah. What grade?"

"Third. You?"

"Same," he said, perching on the seat of his beat-up bike, its frame rusted and dented from too many rainy days and too many failed tricks.

"Maybe we'll be in the same class," Malia said. Her jet-black hair was pulled back, and her dress was a soft brown with white stockings. No other girls in the neighborhood wore stockings. Dillion noticed that. She was different.

"Dillion! Time for dinner!" a voice called from across the street. His mom stood at the door, waving. At the same time, a red sedan pulled into the driveway. Dillion dropped his bike and ran.

Malia watched as his untied laces dragged behind him with every step. He ran straight into his father's arms, laughing, the two of them hugging tightly as his mom snapped a photo from the steps. Malia had never seen that woman without a camera. She seemed to live for capturing joy.

Malia turned away. She wished she had a life worth photographing.

"Malia!" her grandmother's voice floated from the window. She hurried back inside.

"I'm here, Nana. I was just taking out the trash," she said quickly.

"You know I don't want you outside without your mama," Nana said gently, but firmly.

"I know. I'm sorry."

"Did your mother say when she's coming home?"

"She called," Malia said, glancing at the beige house phone beside her. "She's working a double. Someone called out, and since she's new, she has to cover it."

"Wanna watch Court TV with me?" her grandmother asked, reaching for the oversized remote with its worn-out buttons.

"No, I found a book in your library. I want to read for a while."

"What book?"

The Secret Garden," Malia said, pulling the worn hardcover from under her arm.

"Oh, that was my favorite when I was your age," Nana said with a smile, her gaze drifting from the television to her granddaughter.

Malia nodded and slipped into the room that now belonged to her. It wasn't much—just a mattress on the floor, a tall lamp she had to tilt to turn on, and a blanket she kept balled up in the corner; but it was hers.

She curled up under the blanket and opened the book, flipping past the title page. As she began to read, her mind wandered. Not to her father, not to the fire, not even to the fear but to the boy. Dillion. He was kind. His family seemed kind. Maybe, one day, she could have something like that too. Maybe, in all this mess, she could find her secret garden.

"Malia! Where are you?"

Her mother's voice was soft but urgent. A familiar jingle of keys scratched against the doorframe.

"Mom! You're off early!" Malia ran out of her bedroom with the book still in her hand, joy washing over her face.

Her mother set her bag down with a sigh and opened her arms. Malia ran into them, holding on just a little longer than usual.

"Well, no, it *is* a bit late; almost time for bed, baby," Malia's mother said as she slid what looked like a box covered with a cream sheet next to the couch. She set her purse on the counter, exhaustion evident in her posture.

Malia hadn't even realized the time. She'd been completely lost in the pages of *The Secret Garden.* Books did that to her. They pulled her into other worlds and let her become someone else for a while. It was the safest escape she had. And this book, right now, made more sense than her own life.

"How's Mom?" Malia's mother asked as she walked into the kitchen, opening the refrigerator just to stare at the near-empty shelves. She had meant to shop that morning, but the double shift had thrown off everything.

"She was watching TV last time I saw her. I've been in my room reading all day," Malia replied, setting her book down carefully.

"Well, at least you're doing something constructive," her mother said, closing the fridge with a sigh. "I'm sorry I've been working so much lately, baby. I have to build up my hours if I want a permanent spot. But I'm off tomorrow. After I enroll you at your new school, we can do whatever you want."

Malia smiled. "Mom, I *know* you've been working hard. You need to rest. You've gotta get settled too."

Her mother smiled back, eyes soft and tired. "Aww, baby, it's okay; it's life."

She paused, then brightened a little. "I *do* have a surprise for you, though. One of my coworkers thought you might like this. She said her kids didn't appreciate it."

She walked back to the box and gently pulled the cream-colored sheet away. As Malia stepped closer, she heard a soft scratching—tiny claws brushing against cardboard.

"What *is* it?" Malia asked, a small glimmer of delight already appeared in her eyes.

"It's Bunny," her mom said with a grin, lifting the sheet fully to reveal a large, fluffy white rabbit with pink eyes and a huge, cotton-ball tail. Its ears twitched as it sat squished in the box, too big for the space it had been carried in.

"It's perfect, Mom!" Malia gasped.

She reached in to lift it, but the rabbit barely moved. Its tiny legs couldn't support the weight of its big body and round head. It was like a plush toy brought to life, too soft and too heavy to hop away.

"Why is it so big?" she asked, using both arms to scoop the bunny up as best she could.

"Well … from what I was told, my coworker's kids overfed it and never played with it. They left it in the cage all day. It didn't get much exercise," her mother explained, watching Malia cradle the bunny like a baby.

"I'll love it forever and ever," Malia whispered. "Thanks, Mom."

Without another word, she ran off to her room, the bunny pressed to her chest like a precious secret. She curled up on the mattress, tucked the bunny under one arm, and reached for her book on the pillow to continue reading right where she'd left off.

"I think it's time for bed soon, Malia," her mother called gently from the doorway, still in her hospital scrubs and bright pink clogs, silhouetted in the soft hallway light.

"Okay, do I have to take a shower?" Malia asked, still engrossed in the pages of the novel she was nearly finished reading.

"Yes, and put Bunny in the box tonight. We'll get a proper cage for her after school tomorrow. I don't want you to squish her tonight," Malia's mother said, watching her daughter fondly. It felt good to finally see her smile again after days of tears.

Malia shut her book, placing a worn piece of tissue between the pages to mark her spot. She carried Bunny down to the cardboard box by the couch and gently placed her inside.

Her mother turned on the shower and gathered towels from her luggage, the same towels she had hastily packed during their sudden departure. They still smelled like their old home. As she held them, she knew with certainty: they were never going back.

The next morning, sunlight streamed through the dusty windowpane and stirred Malia from her sleep. As soon as the light touched her eyes, she remembered her new friend.

"Hello, Mr. Bunny," she whispered, peeking into the box. Bunny was still sound asleep.

She decided not to wake him. He probably felt the same as she did: displaced, confused, but slowly adjusting.

Her mother walked in, finding Malia on her knees, watching Bunny.

“I think there’s some lettuce in the fridge,” she said.

“He’s asleep. I’ll feed him when he wakes up,” Malia whispered, not wanting to startle her new pet.

“Okay, well, get dressed. I laid some clothes on the bed for you. We need to be at the school by eight,” her mother said, heading to the kitchen to start her morning coffee. The bitter brew lacked cream and sugar—supplies she hadn’t yet replaced.

“You guys up and about?” came a raspy voice from the back room.

“Yup. Do you need anything?” Malia’s mother called back, walking in with a clean bedpan. She helped the elderly woman to the edge of the bed.

“Your nurse will be here shortly to help with your bath and to take you to your appointment. I’ll be back with groceries, and maybe we can go for a ride to get some fresh air.”

Malia dressed in her favorite pink dress, signature stockings, and black school shoes. She waited in the living room while her mother gathered her things.

“You ready? Let’s head out. I have your papers in my purse. We’re all set.”

As they stepped outside toward the old brown station wagon, a cheerful voice called out from across the street.

“Hey! Hello! I’m Dillion’s mom, Tasha. Welcome!”

Layla smiled. “I’m Layla, and this is my daughter Malia.”

"I'm the 'block mom', so if you need anything while you're settling in, don't hesitate to knock," Tasha said, walking over with a warm smile.

"Thank you. We surely will."

"My son's not a morning person; he'll be out in a minute. Are you headed to Steeple Creek now?"

"Yes, it's Malia's first day," Layla replied, just as a young boy emerged from the house, clearly annoyed.

"Mom, what are you doing?" Dillion grumbled.

"And I guess this is Dillion," Layla said, smiling.

"Maybe they'll be in the same class. We can carpool if you'd like. I still walk him to school. It makes me feel better."

"That would be great. I was going to let her walk, but this sounds like a better plan," Layla said, glancing at Malia for approval.

Neither child spoke, but both sensed this would become a routine.

At Steeple Creek Elementary, banners lined the walls: "Let's Go Steeple Creek!" and "Be Your Best Self Every Day!" The scent of pine cleaner and bubble gum filled the air. Malia took in the sound of laughter and sneakers squeaking against the floors. It already felt like a place she could call home.

Dillion led them to the main office.

"This is the office. The principal is Mr. Chris—he's nice," he said, holding the door.

"I have to get to homeroom. Maybe I'll see you later," he added, disappearing down the hall.

"Malia Marsh? We've been expecting you," said a heavy-set woman behind a cluttered desk.

"Yes, ma'am," Malia replied quietly.

"Mr. Chris will be with you in two minutes," she said, taking the papers Layla handed over.

Malia and her mother sat on a bench near the door.

A small man soon emerged, his loud voice contrasting his size.

"Malia, Mom, welcome! I'm Mr. Chris. Let's get Malia to class, shall we? I see your grades are impressive. You'll be in our Cheetah Class, an advanced group."

He led them down the hall to the classroom where Dillion had vanished earlier. Through the window, Malia saw the back of his blond-tipped fauxhawk.

Mr. Chris knocked, then dramatically opened the door.

"Mrs. Simmons, Cheetahs, we have a new addition today—Malia!"

"We've been expecting you! Class, let's welcome our newest Cheetah!" Mrs. Simmons said, turning from the board.

"Welcome, welcome!" the class chimed.

"Your seat is here," she added, pointing to a desk behind Dillion's.

Malia hugged her mother, then took her seat. Her mother and the principal returned to the office to complete paperwork.

This was Malia's third school in two years. But something about this place felt different, like it could be home.

She stared at Dillion's fauxhawk, captivated. She'd never seen a haircut like that before.

At the end of the day, Malia lingered to admire the classroom art and chat with Mrs. Simmons. She slowly made her way to the front door. Outside, she saw Dillion standing at the curb, but something felt off. She scanned the line of cars but didn't see her mother.

Dillion looked up. His mother and Principal Chris were in a serious conversation.

Tasha knelt beside Malia.

"Today, you have to come with me. There's an emergency, and we need to meet your mom," she said, offering her hand.

"What's wrong? Is everything okay?"

"Yes, honey. I just signed you out. Come on, let's go."

They got into the car. Malia's stomach fluttered with worry. Tasha drove with determination, white-knuckled on the wheel.

Malia watched the trees fly by, trying to remember the last time she'd seen the highway in daylight. When she and her mom had fled their home, everything was a blur. Today, the road was sharp and real.

"Where are we going? Are we going back home?"

"No, sweetheart. Your mom will explain everything when we get there."

They exited the highway and pulled into the parking lot of a large building. The sign read: EMERGENCY ROOM ENTRANCE.

Tasha unlocked the doors. Dillion stirred, wiping drool from his cheek.

"Where are we? Are we there yet?" he asked groggily.

Tasha didn't answer. She parked, checked her phone, made a quick call, then led the children inside.

Malia was confused. Her mom worked at this hospital—she remembered the name from the badge she always wore.

They sat in the lobby. Malia's thoughts raced. Why wasn't she home? Was something wrong with Nana? Had her father found them?

Finally, the large wooden door opened, and Layla appeared, still in the same clothes. She rushed to Malia, hugging her so tightly it was hard to breathe. She knelt to thank Tasha, hugging her with genuine gratitude.

"No worries," Tasha said. "Call me when you're ready. You have my number."

"Mom, what's going on?" Malia asked.

"Let's go upstairs. I'll explain on the way."

As they headed to the elevator, Dillion and his mother quietly exited the lobby.

Something was about to change again.

"Mom, are you going to tell me now?"

"Yeah, baby ... it's Nana. She had an accident."

"What's wrong? Did she fall again?"

"Well, we don't quite know yet."

Malia and her mother entered another set of oak doors that opened as soon as they got close enough to smell the scent of freshly sprayed Lysol on the metal trim. They stepped into a corridor filled with computers and monitors, with women seated behind metal desks. After several turns, they stopped at another oak door in the hallway.

"Nana is sleeping right now. Hopefully, she'll wake up soon."

"Is she sleeping, like her afternoon nap?"

"Yeah ... something like that," Malia's mother said, squeezing her hand firmly.

They walked into a brightly lit room. In the center, surrounded by machines that beeped and whistled, Nana lay tethered to each one. White sheets covered her—sheets that reminded Malia of the ones that had draped Bunny's box just the night before. Tubes came from Nana's mouth. A nurse read the monitors and checked Nana's eyes for movement with the tiny light at the end of a pen.

This wasn't just an afternoon nap.

Chapter 3: Warding

In lacrosse, a ward is an illegal move—used to push others away instead of playing with skill and trust. Malia had learned to do the same in life. Especially with her father. As she sat beside Nana's bed, the instinct returned: protect her heart, push him back before he could hurt her again.

Malia sat anxiously in the corner beside her mother. The hours dragged on. Doctors and nurses entered and exited at irregular intervals, checking and rechecking, but Nana remained still. Time passed, and the room grew dimmer. The staff stopped coming. The air turned cooler.

It must be late, Malia thought. She wondered if she'd miss school tomorrow—she had only just started. Her eyelids grew heavy. She curled up next to her mother under a heavy cream-colored sheet. Just as she began to drift off, there was a knock at the door.

"Baby girl?" A familiar whisper floated in before a figure stepped inside.

"Daddy?" Malia's heart warmed at the sight of her father's face. For a brief moment, she forgot all the misery he had caused. But he was still her daddy.

He swung open the door and wrapped her in a hug. Her mother shifted slightly in her seat, clearly unimpressed with his entrance. After holding Malia for a short while, he walked over to his mother's bed and leaned over her motionless body.

"Mama? Mama?" he whispered, as if his voice alone could wake her. "Mama, I'm sorry," he said, bowing his head and grabbing Nana's limp hand.

Malia studied her father's face. She remembered the pain he caused their family—the drinking, the abuse, the nights he didn't come home. Nana had always come to Malia's rescue. She was the fixer. Her father had caused Nana so much stress. Nana blamed herself for the way he turned out, but Malia knew the truth: it was his fault Nana was here.

Malia shrank into the corner next to her mother. They both watched, slightly in awe. Her father was showing genuine compassion, something they had rarely, if ever, seen. This was real. Malia watched tears fill his eyes and wondered what thoughts passed through his mind. She knew what was in hers: anger, a feeling she rarely allowed, but always when it came to him.

Malia clutched the blanket tighter. It now served as a barrier between her and her father. It wouldn't stop him, but it was something. Her father stepped into the hallway and returned with a black rolling chair. He placed it beside the bed, sat down, and held Nana's hand in his own.

"Mother, please forgive me," he muttered, then began whispering the Lord's Prayer. In that moment, it was like no one else existed in the room.

"Too late now. The damage is done," Layla whispered. She thought it was to herself, but Malia heard and understood.

Just as he finished the prayer, the machines around Nana let out a series of rebellious beeps. Everyone stood. The doors flew open, lights came on, and hospital staff rushed in.

Malia and her parents were ushered into the hallway. As they passed through the doorway, all Malia could hear was the machines and someone calling, "Clear!" followed by a loud electric charge.

"Nana!" she screamed as her mother pulled her close in the hallway.

"It's okay, baby," her mother whispered, stroking her cheeks gently to comfort her.

Layla knew what was happening. She had prepared for this moment. She knew it was the end of Nana's journey. In her head, she thought no eight-year-old should ever have to digest something like this. But in her heart, she knew it was necessary for Malia's journey.

While they waited in the hallway, Layla slipped her phone from her pocket and sent a few quick texts. Soon, the oak doors opened again, and a small woman walked toward them carrying a bundle in her arms. She stopped at Malia's feet. It was Bunny.

"Malia, he missed you a lot. He almost clawed through the box," the woman said, hugging Malia and then her mother.

"I already made the arrangements. You're on leave until further notice. Take your time," she told Layla.

Malia buried her face in Bunny's soft fur. Tears soaked the rabbit's coat like morning dew on leaves. The machines fell silent. The doctors stepped out. Nana was gone.

The air felt still. No one could look Malia in the eye. She looked up and spotted her father at the far end of the hall, watching her. He looked as if he had lost twenty pounds in an instant. His face appeared long and solemn, hands shoved deep in his pockets. The doctors approached him. He collapsed to his knees.

No one needed to tell Malia that the woman who had saved her so many times from the monster had left, and that the monster was the one who slayed her.

"Aren't the good guys supposed to win?" she thought.

Malia clutched Bunny as her mother led her into a room next to where Nana had once been. They sat at a small wooden table and said nothing. The only sound was sniffles and the quiet fall of tears down their cheeks.

Malia didn't go to school the next morning. She stayed in bed with Bunny. Her mother brought boxes in and began packing up items from Nana's room, gathering papers.

Nana had left everything to Malia, her only other blood relative. She'd made those arrangements after her first brush with death. When Malia's father had tried to sell the house during that first illness, thinking he'd inherit her wealth, Nana recovered and made sure he'd never have that kind of power again.

Malia, unaware of everything she now owned, lay on her bed with Bunny. The sun shone outside, but her heart was cloudy, and tears rained down on her pillow. She imagined how her day might've gone if Nana were still alive. She saw herself walking the school hallways, meeting new kids, learning something unexpected from Mrs. Simmons and, most of all, watching the blonde-tipped mohawk in front of her.

She wondered what Dillion was doing.

"Malia, baby," her mother called.

"Yes, ma'am?" she replied, wiping her tears on the bedsheet.

"You have visitors," her mother said, her voice tinged with excitement.

Malia checked the clock—just after noon. Who could it be? Everyone was supposed to be at school or work. Her father wouldn't dare show up—not now. She cracked her door and peeked into the hallway. All she could see was sunlight streaming through the open front door and a few silhouettes.

"Hey, this is for you," Dillion said, handing her a giant basket filled with candy and chocolates, wrapped in a pastel bow. Clearly, his mother had made it.

"Thank you. Was there no school today?" she asked, struggling to hold the oversized gift. He quickly reconsidered and placed it on the couch.

"No. I didn't feel that great this morning. Mom kept me home," he said, avoiding eye contact—his gaze fixed on some invisible point in the air. Afraid to admit the real reason he stayed home.

"If you're up to it… and you decide to go to school tomorrow, we'll pick you up," Dillion's mother said, trying to ease the tension in her son's voice.

"Thank you. I don't want to miss school. I've already missed a lot at my old one," Malia replied, warmed by the thought of seeing them at her front door in the morning.

In that moment, Malia realized Dillion might be the support she never knew she needed. The kind she'd never truly had. He was going to be her *forever* friend.

Chapter 4: The Clear

A "clear" in lacrosse is when the defending team successfully transitions the ball from their defensive end to the offensive end, shifting from pressure to opportunity. It's fast, strategic, and vital—much like the turning point Malia and Dillion are about to experience.

Malia looked down from the stands, eyes tracking Dillion as he sliced across the field. He weaved between defenders with speed and precision, his stick a natural extension of his body. Lacrosse was his first love. Football and basketball were hobbies, but the field—this field—was home.

He was a force. The reigning Catholic School Player of the Year three years running. Media outlets called him "The LeBron James of Lacrosse." But to Dillion and his dad, he was Ricky Bobby— *"If you ain't first, you're last."* A quote from their favorite movie.

"Shake and bake, Dillion!" his father yelled proudly, seated next to Malia.

The three of them—Dillion's father, his mom, and Malia—always tried to attend the games together. It had become tradition. Family, even. That's what Dillion's mom always said whenever someone asked how Malia fit into the picture. *"They found each other."* Malia smiled at the thought.

She attended Bryant's Mar, an elite all-girls prep school just ten minutes away from Dillion's. Student government president, Honor Society member, and soon-to-be valedictorian. College offers flooded in, but she hadn't made her final decision yet. She had one month left. Coincidentally, so did Dillion.

He went to Garçon Academy, an all-boys school his father insisted on to keep him focused. Dillion was sharp. Not in the academic sense like Malia, but clever, observant, and relentless. His school protected him like a treasure; he was their golden boy, their claim to fame.

“Good game, Crabs!” Malia shouted as the final whistle blew. The name still made her cringe. A giant red crab as a mascot? Probably a nod to Maryland’s seafood legacy, she figured, though blue crabs were more accurate. Still, for a school as prestigious as Garçon, she expected better. But she always overthought those things.

The team raised their claws—thumb and fingers clamped together—and jogged off the field like a swarm of crustaceans. Dillion, of course, was last. Reporters swarmed him.

“Dillion, incredible game! What’s the mindset going into next week’s championship?” a reporter asked, microphone up.

“We face these guys every year. They always find ways to surprise us,” Dillion said, media-trained and polished.

“If you win, that’s your fourth title. How does this one compare?”

“I play every game the same—hard, fast, and for the team. No regrets.”

He wiped the sweat, black war paint now running down his cheeks, and looked up at the stands. A subtle signal. Time to make his own clear from the media spotlight to something real.

“Where are we going to celebrate?” Dillion asked his dad.

“Home,” his father said, already walking off.

“I made tacos; it’s taco night,” his mother added, folding her seat and grabbing her ridiculous crab hat.

"I'm riding with you," Malia told them. "My car's in the shop. Got a ride here."

Dillion stayed on the field, lacrosse stick in hand, grinning through exhaustion. The fame never impressed his family. They loved him too much to let it change him. That was their kind of clear: keep it grounded, stay humble, move forward.

He jogged to the car and spotted Malia already in the passenger seat.

"Toss me the keys!" she called out.

"You're not driving! That's why your car's always in the shop—you *can't* drive."

"Whatever," she said, laughing as she opened the driver's door from the inside. It had been busted since his dad's infamous "accident". Dillion loved the car anyway.

"You really need to fix that door," Malia said, fighting with her seatbelt.

"It's fine. If I trade anything in, it'll be *you*," he joked. They both burst into laughter.

They turned down the street they'd driven together every day for the last nine years. They passed Malia's house and pulled into Dillion's driveway.

"Oh, shoot—I forgot to feed Bunny!" Malia said as she jumped out, slamming the rusted red door behind her.

"Just call your mom and have her do it. It's taco night, and I'm starving," Dillion groaned.

"She's working all night."

"Okay, I'll walk you down."

They walked to the house Dillion had come to think of as his second home. It looked nothing like the place he remembered from their childhood. The walls were freshly painted, the floors lined with crown molding, and the furniture modern and handpicked, after hours of Malia dragging him to every store imaginable.

When they entered her room, Dillion glanced at the plush sleigh bed and the new curtains. He smiled, remembering the mattress that used to sit on the floor, next to a single lamp.

"Bunny's still ticking. I think he might hold the record for the world's oldest bunny," he joked.

"Yeah. Bunny's a soldier. He might outlive us both."

Malia scattered pellets into the bedding of Bunny's cage. The rabbit twitched his nose, slowly lumbering over like an elderly man looking for his glasses.

They watched him eat.

"Let's go, I'm starving," Dillion said as his stomach growled.

"Okay. Let me grab my overnight stuff; I'm staying with you tonight. You can quiz me for my physics exam and drop me off in the morning."

"So, when were you going to ask me? I could've had a hot date!" Dillion teased, ushering her out of the room.

Malia rolled her eyes. "You don't have plans. You never do."

She was right. She always was. She knew everything about him, every habit, every secret. Dillion was her brother in everything but blood.

They reached his front door, dropped their bags in the hallway, and were instantly greeted by the smell of seasoned turkey and toasted taco shells. His parents were already seated, surrounded by an array of toppings that could rival any taco bar.

“Where’s Bunny?” his mom asked as she pulled the shells from the oven.

“He’s cranky when I move him. I think I’ll keep him home until I can get him to the vet.”

“Aww, poor thing,” she said, pausing with concern.

“Can we eat now? I’m starving,” his dad interjected, unmoved by bunny-related crisis. He often said feeding his family was enough responsibility without adding pets to the mix.

The four of them sat down to eat. Normally, his mom kicked off dinner with some wild news story from the internet. Tonight, she had a different plan.

“Sooo … prom is coming up,” she said casually. “What are you two doing?”

Dillion, mid-bite, nearly choked on his taco.

“I don’t do prom, Mom. It’s a bunch of yuppies showing off their emperor’s new clothes.”

“I haven’t really thought about it,” Malia added. “Been too busy trying to finish my volunteer hours.”

"I think every girl should go to prom. You'll regret it if you don't," his mom insisted. "I'll help with the dress! And pictures!"

Dillion and Malia exchanged a look as they began clearing the table.

"I think you should go," Dillion said, running water for the dishes. "Mom's right."

"Are you going to yours?"

"Nope. But you should go. All you do is study and do service work. You'll be a nun by the time you're twenty."

"I'll go when you go."

"I'll go to yours, but not mine. Deal?" He dumped soap into the sink.

Malia looked up from the table. "You're serious, aren't you? You want to go but you're using me as an excuse."

"I'll check it out. I mean, it's our last shot. And if the girls at your school are anything like you—mouthy and stubborn—it'll be a blast."

Malia glanced toward the living room, where the TV had gone unusually quiet. The clicking of crochet needles had also stopped.

"Fine. Get your camera ready," she called out loudly. "And you're paying for the dress!"

"Deal!" came the small voice from the next room.

Later, Dillion's dad wandered in for his evening tea and a customary kitchen inspection.

"If you two are serious, we'll handle the incidentals," he said.

"What do you mean, 'incidentals'?" Dillion asked, skeptical.

"Dress. Tux. We got it."

"Limo? Dinner?"

"You've got a car. And the prom's on taco night."

"Can you at least get the tickets?" Dillion shouted as his dad disappeared up the stairs. Silence.

The night wound down with showers, comfy clothes, and their usual study routine in the family den. Their playlist was a mix of R&B and country, a tribute to Dillion's mom's childhood influences.

"You almost done? I need you to quiz me," Malia said after her favorite song ended.

"You've got twenty minutes before I watch film and get my beauty sleep," he replied with a smirk.

Malia gave him a look. He still had that same crooked smile, though now he wore it on a chiseled face. His shaggy hair, an attempted surfer look, curled just below his ears—more wave than surf. He'd grown into an athlete, lean and strong, but to her, he was still the boy with the fauxhawk who jumped on mattresses.

She crawled over with her notes.

"Okay, ask me these. I'll write the answers down. Just tell me when you're ready."

Oh, wait, I have the perfect idea on where to host the prom.

The idea to host prom at Sammy's Trattoria came to Malia while scrolling through photos from a friend's birthday dinner on

Instagram. The cozy, tucked-away restaurant with its string lights, brick walls, and old-world charm felt different—warm, real. Not some soulless school gym with a rented DJ and folding chairs.

She brought it up one night at dinner.

"I was thinking," Malia said, stirring her rice in a circle, "what if prom wasn't at the school this year?"

Layla, her mother, glanced up. "What do you mean?"

"I mean, what if we had it somewhere better? Somewhere with actual food, and ambiance. Somewhere like Sammy's."

Her mom raised a brow. "You want to throw prom at an Italian restaurant?"

"It's not *just* a restaurant. It's part of the community. Everyone knows Sammy. And he loves hosting events. He did Aunt Rena's retirement party, remember?"

Layla smiled. "I remember. And you're thinking of organizing it?"

"With a team, yeah. I already have ideas. Lighting, music, food. I just need to talk to him."

The next afternoon, Malia walked into the trattoria and found Sammy behind the counter, rolling dough and humming to Frank Sinatra.

"Malia!" he boomed, wiping his hands on his apron. "I was just thinking about your mother. How is she?"

"She's good. And she told me to tell you to stop using so much salt in the eggplant parm."

Sammy threw his head back in laughter. "Tell her I'll cut it down when she starts eating meat again."

Malia grinned. "I actually came to ask you something."

Sammy leaned in, hands on the counter. "Go on."

"What would you think about hosting this year's prom here? Just a few dozen students, good food, some lights. I'd handle the details."

For a moment, Sammy didn't speak. Then he placed a hand over his heart.

"Malia, you want to bring your memories here. That means something to me. Of course. We'll make this place sparkle. But you plan it right, no half-hearted jobs."

"You got it," she said, already imagining the layout. "No folding chairs."

Sammy pointed. "No glitter on my ravioli."

Later that night, Malia shared the update with Dillion while they walked Bunny in his backyard.

"So, Sammy's in," she said.

"Great. I can already see it—me spilling tomato sauce down my tux."

Malia rolled her eyes. "We're not eating in our outfits."

Dillion's mom, Tasha, was watering her plants nearby and overheard.

"Sammy's doing prom now?" she asked, eyebrows raised.

"It was Malia's idea," Dillion said, tossing a stick. "Apparently the gym is too basic."

Tasha turned to Malia with a smile. "That's actually brilliant. And Sammy will do it right. Just let me know what you need. I can help coordinate desserts or flowers or... whatever."

"Thanks, Ms. Tasha," Malia said. "I might take you up on that."

Later that evening, Layla sat on the edge of Malia's bed, flipping through a binder her daughter had already filled with sketches and notes.

"You really want to pull this off?"

"Yeah," Malia said. "I don't want it to feel like just another school night with fancy clothes. I want it to matter."

Layla gave her a long look, proud but slightly misty-eyed. "You're growing up fast, you know that?"

"Don't get soft," Malia warned.

Layla laughed. "I'm just saying. You're taking something simple and turning it into something beautiful."

"Well," Malia replied, smiling softly, "Sammy's doing the heavy lifting. I'm just trying to bring some magic."

Layla squeezed her hand. "You already are."

Chapter 5: The Ride

In lacrosse, "the ride" is a test of grit—pressuring the opponent as they try to clear the ball, forcing a turnover, fighting for one more chance. Tonight, everything felt like a ride. This was more than a game. It was Dillion's last chance in his school's jersey, his final run with the brothers he'd bled with. Under the lights of Homewood Field—where childhood memories and future dreams collided—he carried the weight of it all: his team, his legacy, and Malia's faith in him.

The day had arrived, the championship game. The air at Johns Hopkins University's Homewood Field buzzed with electricity. A sea of crimson and navy poured into the stadium, filling the stands with the raucous energy of devoted families, alumni, and student sections chanting their school's names. The sun dipped behind the skyline, casting golden hues across the turf, with stadium lights humming to life above.

For Dillion, this wasn't just a game. It was home. He'd come to Homewood as a child, running along the perimeter track with sticky ice cream fingers and his father's firm hand on his shoulder. He remembered idolizing the players; those giants of speed and strength who danced with sticks like wands. For the last three years, Dillion had been one of them. More than that, he had become known as the King of Homewood, an MVP every year, and the heartbeat of his team, the Crabs.

But now, sitting in the locker room beneath the humming fluorescent lights, Dillion was quiet. Headphones on. His head bowed. His palms cradled the cleats he'd written his parents' names on: "Stay Humble," scrawled in black Sharpie down the soles. Three sticks strung and ready. Pads aligned. Socks folded neatly. He needed everything to be perfect.

“You ready?” Coach Simmons' voice rumbled into the room. His towering frame filled the doorway, his eyes scanning the locker room packed with adrenaline and fear. Players taped ankles and bounced knees nervously to music. Dillion raised his head.

“Dillion, I need you today. Today is the day,” Coach said, gripping the back of his neck. “I know it’s big but just remember it’s still the same game. It’s just the last time you’ll wear this jersey.”

Dillion nodded. “I know, Coach.”

“Listen, I know you’re undecided on schools. But Georgetown’s here today. They want you—bad.”

“Georgetown, huh?” Dillion raised an eyebrow.

Coach chuckled. “Yeah, I know. Preppy. But still Maryland’s only two hours away. Full ride. They see what I see.”

Dillion smirked. “Coach, I’m a blue-collar kid with swag. I barely blend with the local prep boys. Georgetown? Man, that’s a different planet.”

“We’ll talk after the game,” Coach said, giving a firm pat to his helmet.

The mood shifted. Headphones slipped off. Laces tied tight. Shoulder pads clicked into place. Then, the sound of cleats against concrete echoed like a war march as the Crabs funneled into the tunnel, faces painted, eyes wild. Chants began—loud, raw, ancient. This wasn’t just sport. It was battle.

Dillion led the charge into the stadium.

The sky overhead was a canvas of twilight purples and blues. The field shimmered under the lights. Crimson warmups fanned across the turf like fire.

As the players stretched in rhythm, Dillion moved from teammate to teammate, grabbing each helmet and looking them in the eyes. "This is our time," he said again and again, pouring belief into their veins.

In the stands, his parents and Malia found their seats. His dad stood tall, arms folded, eyes trained on the field like a general inspecting his troops. His mother, as always, had red pom-poms in her hair as a tradition. Malia, calm and observant, watched Dillion. She was proud. Nervous. Protective.

The coin was tossed. Dillion and the other two captains locked arms and jogged to midfield. They were the last of the seniors still standing.

The referee raised his whistle. "Let's keep it clean. Shot clock by discretion. Good luck."

The whistle blew. Countdown started. Teams to sidelines.

Opening Faceoff.

Dillion crouched low, his stick angled for war. The rival middie mirrored his stance.

Whistle.

The ball snapped into the mesh of both crosses. A brutal tangle. For seconds, it was primal. Then, the rival came away with it. A swift transition. A shot.

Goal. 1–0. Barely thirty seconds in. Dillion didn't flinch.

Another faceoff. Another grind. Another goal for the opponent. 2–0.

Coach Simmons signaled a timeout, jaw tight.

In the huddle, his voice thundered. “You ready to show up?”

“Yes, sir!”

“Then do it! Dillion—go to the wing. Let Alexander face off.”

The substitutions were a shock. Dillion accepted it, jaw clenched. The other team was faster, tighter, and came to the field with a plan—to crush him first.

Another faceoff. Another goal. 3–0.

Malia watched nervously. Dillion’s father leaned so far forward it looked like he might fall from the bleachers. His eyes tracked every pass, every cut, every failure.

4–0. Halftime.

The Crabs sat in stunned silence. Sweat dripped. Chests heaved.

Coach Simmons hurled his hat. “Who the hell is gonna step up?! You look like a JV squad out there!”

Plays changed. Bench players rotated in. Dillion sat watching. His team battled back. A goal. Then another. 4–2. Dillion cheered from the sideline, slapping backs, offering water. But it felt hollow. He wasn’t used to being powerless.

Then came the call. “Dillion, get hot!”

Two minutes left. Down by one. He raced to the substitution box, called off his sub, and took the field. This was it. They cleared space. Isolation play. All on Dillion. 30 seconds.

He dodged from the alley, crossed the face of the goal. Three defenders closed. He faked high, dipped low and fired. The ball shot between the goalie's legs.

GOAL**.** Tie game.

The crowd erupted. His team sprinted toward him.

But then, the referee waved it off: crease violation, no goal. Game over.

The field blurred. Dillion fell to his knees. Around him, chaos. Screams. Cheers. Teammates. Referees. A tunnel of sound. He stared at the black rubber pellets of the turf.

Coach Simmons knelt beside him: "I know it hurts. But finish this right. Lead them back."

Dillion stood, eyes glassy. He returned to the locker room. A crypt. He dropped to his knee. One by one, his team joined him.

"This one's on me," he said. "You guys gave everything. We were a family. I love you guys. Take it back next year. For all of us." Emotion choked his voice.

Coach stepped in, "You didn't get outplayed. I got outcoached. You left it all on the field."

One last chant. One last prayer. Season over.

Outside, the field emptied. The last buses waited.

Dillion’s mother hugged him tightly. His father placed a strong hand on his shoulder, silent.

Then came Malia: “That was still the best game of the year,” she said softly. “You’ll play more. You’ll win more.”

Dillion didn’t answer.

She walked beside him to the SUV. It was taco night, but no one would eat. Not tonight.

Chapter 6: Holding

In lacrosse, holding, or illegally keeping someone from moving forward, is a penalty. Dillion was doing the same; trapped by pressure, expectations, and a dream he wasn't sure was his. And the harder he tried to hold it all together, the more it pulled him apart.

Several days had passed, and Dillion was still a shell of himself—sulking, drifting through classes, going through the motions with just enough energy to keep his mother from worrying. But those who knew him could see it; his usual sharpness was gone, replaced with a dull haze.

When Dillion got home from school that Friday afternoon, his father was waiting in the family room, a folded newspaper resting between his knees.

"Dillion, what's up?"

"Nothing. Just gonna head upstairs and chill," Dillion replied, trying to escape.

"Can we talk?" his father asked, his tone calm but direct.

Dillion hesitated, then dropped his bag by the door and sank into the two-seater couch across from his father's old recliner, the one no one else was allowed to sit in.

His dad spoke before Dillion could fully settle. "How long are you going to let this get to you?"

"I'm fine," Dillion said, smugly brushing it off. "What are you even talking about?"

"Life is bigger than lacrosse, son. There'll be plenty more losses out there in the real world. It's what you do with them and how you grow from them, that matters."

Dillion met his father's eyes, a familiar glaze forming. "That's what you say to losers. I've heard that speech since I was ten."

He rose his voice: "If it's just about learning from losing, then why have me train for hours every week? Why sacrifice my time, my energy, my social life—for what? Lacrosse and studying. That's it."

His father exhaled. "I just wanted to help you succeed. You've only lost one championship in four years; that's not a bad record."

"But I gave everything for this! If I'm going to commit my life to something, I need to win every time. I need to be perfect. That's the pressure I live with."

His father leaned forward. "Is there something else going on? Because it feels like this is bigger than just one game."

Dillion looked away, his voice quieting. "Don't you wonder why I haven't picked a school yet? I don't know what I want. I don't even know if I want to do this anymore."

"I thought you were just waiting to see where Malia would end up," his father said, confused.

Dillion stood up. "Do you know how much pressure I'm under to make the right decision? To keep everyone happy? I know you'll say it's my choice, but it hasn't felt like my choice in years. We've all been chasing this dream, but I'm starting to think it's not mine."

His father's face tightened, but he stayed calm. "We just wanted you to have the best opportunities—"

"Yeah, *your* best. I've seen the Georgetown letters on your desk. I know Coach has been calling. You never even told me."

"I didn't want to distract you before the season ended. I was collecting information so you could make the best choice when you were ready."

"Or so you could make it for me," Dillion shot back. "Do you even know if lacrosse is my favorite sport? You never asked."

The room fell into silence. Dillion grabbed his bag and walked to the door. His father rose to follow, but by the time he stood, the door had slammed shut.

Dillion didn't know where else to go. So he went to the only other place that felt like home—Malia's.

She was at her desk, finishing a paper, when she heard a soft knock on her window. Dillion. She opened it and he whispered, "Come open the front door."

By the time she met him downstairs, he was already at the porch, looking unsettled.

"What's going on?" she asked as she opened the door.

"We need to talk," he said, brushing past her.

Dillion never said that. He rarely talked about his feelings—only sports, mostly lacrosse. But now he sprawled across her bed, tossing pillows aside, burying his face into them like a boy trying to disappear.

"Can I ask you something?" he mumbled.

"Of course," she said, returning to her desk but keeping an eye on him.

“What’s your dream? I mean ... what do you actually want to do with your life?”

She paused. “Right now? I’m trying to find a college program I love and stay close to home, if I can. Is that what you mean?”

“No. I mean your *dream*. What drives you?”

Malia turned to face him fully. “I’ve always seen myself teaching or doing something that matters. Making a difference. Helping people realize their own potential.”

She giggled. “Why? You lose one game and now you’re getting all philosophical?”

But then she noticed he wasn’t smiling. A single tear traced the curve of his cheek as he stared silently at the ceiling.

“I don’t feel like I’m living my own life,” he whispered. “No one’s ever asked what I wanted. They just assume I’m the same Dillion I was at ten; that I still want what I used to want.”

The words poured out, fast and clumsy like they’d been trapped inside for too long. Malia shut her laptop and rolled her chair to the side of the bed.

“What is this really about?” she asked softly.

“I don’t know if I can keep doing this for another four years. Train every day. Perform. Make sure the team wins. Make the school look good. Please my parents. Please everyone but me. I feel like ... like a slave to it.”

Tears streamed now, unchecked. He turned his back to her, burying his face into the pillow.

"Is that why you haven't committed to a school yet?" she asked gently, backing off just enough to give him space.

"I guess," he said. "I just don't know what it feels like to want something for *me*."

Malia stood and slowly pulled a blanket over him. "Well, prom is next week. Let's just focus on that, okay? One thing at a time. Plus, our parents already paid for everything, might as well look good."

"Okay," he murmured.

She turned back to her laptop, letting the soft sound of typing fill the room. He drifted off behind her, finally at peace, at least for now.

Dillion pulled himself up to the headboard, squinting toward the window. The light cut across the room like a blade. He glanced at the clock; 8:00 a.m. He wandered out and found Malia curled up on the living room couch, a blanket half-sliding off her shoulder.

"Morning. You definitely got some beauty sleep," she muttered, eyes half-open. "I tried to wake you up last night to get a shower, your dirty butt was all up in my sheets."

Dillion gave a sheepish grin. "Sorry. What time are we going to get fitted?"

Malia sat up and yawned. "My mom ran out to grab breakfast. Once she gets back, she's taking us, then we're meeting your mom at the boutique."

"What about my dad?"

Malia shrugged. "Didn't say anything about him."

She turned back to scrolling through the TV menu. Her eyes landed on a familiar title and her face lit up.

"Oh! Found it!"

Her voice jumped with excitement. It was her favorite survival reality show, the one where contestants were dropped into desolate wilderness and forced to band together to survive.

"I love this show."

Dillion dropped onto the couch beside her. "You wouldn't last five minutes out there."

"I'd last longer than you. You're spoiled. Your dear mommy can't make you tacos in the wild," she teased.

They both laughed, the sound echoing in the quiet morning.

As the show played, Dillion's gaze drifted to the screen. Something about the simplicity of it—the raw need to survive—struck him. No expectations. No college decisions. Just you and the elements. Do or die.

The door lock clicked. Keys jangled. Dillion jumped up and opened the door. Malia's mom, Layla, stood on the other side juggling three large paper bags.

"Thanks, Dillion," she said as he took them from her arms.

"Poultry-Filet—my favorite," Dillion grinned, digging for a chicken biscuit as he headed to the kitchen.

"Eat quick," Layla called out. "We've got to meet your mom at the boutique."

She tossed the blanket off Malia and snatched the remote.

"Wait—Mom! They're about to catch the caribou!" Malia twisted her body, trying to keep the TV in view.

Layla rolled her eyes. "Spoiler alert: they don't. They end up sharing berries and frog guts. This episode's old. Let's go; TV off."

They scarfed down breakfast and rushed to get ready. Soon, the trio was in Layla's car, cruising through the city toward the boutique.

Dillion's thoughts began to drift. He wondered if his dad had been thinking about what he'd said during their last conversation. Usually, his father would've checked in by now and tried to talk it out. Maybe this time was different.

They arrived at the boutique, familiar but still unfamiliar. They'd come once before, more out of obligation than expertise. Neither had ever been to a formal event like prom, especially not together.

Dillion changed into his tuxedo, adjusting the jacket with careful precision. It fit better than he expected—slim but not tight, just enough room to breathe.

He waited for his mother. Ten minutes passed. She finally walked in.

"Mom, everything okay?" he asked, catching the slight delay.

"Yeah. Just lost track of time," she replied, shifting her black-and-grey houndstooth purse from her right shoulder to the left. A small habit, but one Dillion knew meant something was off.

"I know you're excited about the prom and all," he said, adjusting his collar, "but I need to know what's going on."

She looked at him, then turned toward a display of silk corsages, feigning interest.

"It's just something you and your father need to talk about—when you're ready."

"I don't know what else to say to him. I think I said it all last time."

His mother looked over her shoulder. "Did you tell him you're planning to visit a campus without him?"

Dillion stiffened. "It's my life. I think I have the latitude to make that choice."

She didn't turn around. "The school called. Asked if we were coming for a photo op."

"Oh."

"If you're leaning toward Maryland, fine. But your father's always been in your corner. You could at least tell him."

From behind the dressing partition, Malia emerged. She wore her dress for the first time in front of Dillion—an elegant silhouette in a shade that perfectly complemented his tux. They had no idea what the other was wearing; their parents had kept them separated for the surprise.

She narrowed her eyes.

"So, when were you going to tell *me*, Dillion?"

His jaw clenched. "We can talk about it later."

The boutique attendant's eyes darted around the room like she was watching a tennis match.

They finished their fittings, purchased the outfits, and zipped them neatly into garment bags. As they filed into the parking lot, Dillion's mother turned to him.

"You coming home now?"

"I'll ride with Malia. I'll be over in a few."

As the seatbelt slid across his chest, Dillion noticed how it pressed against his collarbone: snug, functional, protective ... and uncomfortable. Like his parents' love, always there and meant to keep him safe. But sometimes it rubbed the wrong way.

He stared out the window.

His life had always been structured: work hard, study, win. The idea of freedom—of choosing something outside of the plan—had always felt ... forbidden. But now, he wasn't so sure.

Were the kids with no structure really lost? Or were they just brave enough to define life on their own terms?

His mind swirled.

"What are you thinking about?" Malia nudged his arm.

"Nothing," he lied.

She saw through it but let it go.

"You need to relax. Prom is in three days. Just enjoy it. You've been so tense lately."

Dillion nodded slowly. "I just ... I think I need to talk to Dad. Clear the air."

Layla glanced at them through the rearview mirror. “Yeah. Talk to him, Dillion. He’s not the easiest man, but communication makes things less heavy. He wants the best for you, that’s all.”

The car turned sharply. They were back in their cul-de-sac. Home.

Dillion stepped out with his garment bag slung over his shoulder, the grey fabric brushing his hand. He watched his mother pull into their driveway. His legs felt heavy, but he took the first step. Toward home. Toward truth. Toward whatever came next.

“When you finish, come over so we can make sure we finish planning.”

Malia knew that Dillion shouldn’t be alone now; she knew his thoughts were eating him up inside. For the first time, she felt distant from her lifelong friend.

Dillion walked up the driveway and reached into his pocket for his keys. His mother’s car wasn’t there; he figured she was at the store getting materials for her crochet orders. She’d received a lot of orders for crochet cactuses. It was warm out, but somewhere in the world, people still wanted her crafts.

Dillion slowly turned the key in the door and stepped into the foyer. The house was eerily quiet. His father was usually in the living room at this time of day, enjoying a cold case drama.

Dillion heard a faint sound from the basement—a TV. His father hadn’t been down there watching TV in years.

As Dillion crept down the steps, the sounds became clearer—cheering, and then his mother’s voice yelling his name from the television. His father was watching old videos of Dillion playing rec league lacrosse. He could hear his mother’s voice yelling encouragement, and the murmur of other parents talking in the background.

Dillion walked into the room and sat next to his father. His father's focus never left the screen.

As they both watched, the camera—shaky and jumping with every good play—focused on young Dillion. In the background, he saw his father looming over the team on the sideline, pacing and coaching. Dillion watched as his father ran up and down the field, almost willing the kids to catch and throw the ball.

He remembered that time clearly. When his father coached him, he gave everything. Not just to him but to all the kids who needed help. He coached for the right reasons, but Dillion always knew that deep down, his father wanted to make him just a little bit better than the rest.

It's only natural, Dillion figured, for a father to want to coach his son's team to know his strengths, his weaknesses. In a way, Dillion was an extension of him.

On screen, the kids fumbled passes and stumbled in their gear. As they watched, Dillion's father silently poured brandy into a snifter.

"All I want is for you to be successful, Dillion," his father said as he brought the glass to his lips.

Dillion noticed the redness in his father's cheeks and the swelling in his bare toes—a sign the alcohol had already settled into his system. How long had he been down here? What was really going on?

"I know, Dad."

"You know why I encouraged you to play lacrosse?"

"Not really. Because I was good at it, I guess."

"I remember when we took you to your first clinic. You were four. I had seen a high school game a few nights before, and the announcer was rattling off college names like Yale, Harvard, Princeton. I thought, *there's gotta be more to this*. So, we signed you up. First day, the coach pulled me aside and said if you stuck with it, you'd be a beast."

He paused, taking a long sip.

"I didn't think much of it at the time, but that coach planted a seed. Bigger than I knew."

"What do you mean?" Dillion asked.

"I figured if I could be there for you—unlike my father—I could help you become more than I ever was. That's why I started coaching. To make sure I could guide you."

"I thought you genuinely loved the game," Dillion said. "Now you're telling me you coached just for me?"

"I started coaching because I knew no one would have your back like I would. This world isn't fair, Dillion. But through you, I did fall in love with the game. I loved the kids, the competition, the community. I sacrificed for you—for lacrosse. For this family."

Dillion listened. He knew his father needed to get this off his chest.

His father hadn't touched a drink in years, not since Dillion was a kid. Back then, the bottle had been a barrier: to school functions, to family time, to peace.

Dillion remembered the way his mom used to hide the liquor bottles. How he'd once asked his father if every drink he saw him with was alcohol. He remembered how, not long after that, the drinking stopped. No ceremony. No big moment. Just ... stopped. His father never talked about it, but Dillion noticed how his mom would watch him closely whenever someone offered a drink at parties.

"So why didn't you ever play?" Dillion asked. "If you loved it so much, why didn't you try it? You played other sports in college."

"Lacrosse is for people someone had a plan for. Nobody had a plan for me, but I had one for you."

He sipped his drink and continued, "Anyone can bounce a basketball or throw a football, but lacrosse? To cradle that ball, to shoot it right? That takes time. Attention. No one gave that to me, so I gave it to you. But this ain't about me, it's about you."

"Is it?" Dillion asked. "Why haven't you ever asked me what I wanted to do?"

The voices on the TV faded into the background. Dillion's father poured another glass. The sound of the liquid hitting ice was sharp in the silence.

"So," his father said. "What do you want to do, son?"

"I'm not sure I want to play anymore."

"That's not what I asked. What's your plan?"

"I want to maybe take a year off. Maybe go abroad. Or just ... be a regular student."

"So why Maryland? Is it because Malia's planning to go there?"

"No. I've always liked Maryland. But I don't know if I want to keep playing ... or practicing … or having every day mapped out. I have no friends outside of you and Malia.

My life's been your plan. I think it's time I figure out mine."

His father sighed but wasn't angry. More ... tired.

"Don't take too long figuring it out. Life moves fast, son. I just want what's best for you. But you don't have forever to decide."

Dillion checked his phone. Evening had crept in.

"If you're serious," his father added, "you should at least let the people who helped you know. Call your coach. Be honest."

"I will."

Dillion walked upstairs, through the quiet house, and stepped outside.

He turned back to look at the place he'd lived his whole life. But it didn't feel the same. The trim was cracked. The steps slanted slightly. Had it always been like that? Or was he just seeing it clearly for the first time?

He crossed the street to his second home and knocked twice before using his key.

"Malia? Where are you?"

"In my room…"

He walked past the living room—no sign of her mother, just the quiet rustle of Bunny in his cage.

In Malia's room, he collapsed onto the bed with a heavy thump.

She swiveled in her chair. "You okay?"

"Yeah, I guess. I'm just done living for other people. I just want to be ... average."

"No, you don't. You just want something different right now. That's normal."

"I'm serious. I want to see what life is like outside of everything I know."

"So, everything you've worked for? You want to just start over?"

"I've been living someone else's dream. Not mine."

"Whose dream, then?"

"My father's."

"Sooo … what's yours?"

"I don't know. That's what I plan to find out. I want to go to Maryland with you. Study. Walk around campus. Go to frat parties. You know … live the dream."

Malia turned her chair back toward the screen. "So, you want to go where I go?"

"I figured you always know what you want. You have a plan. I'll just follow your lead until my vision shows up. Until my purpose finds me."

"I don't think that's a good idea, Dillion. I think you're just having a pre-midlife crisis. A 'middie-life' crisis."

Dillion laughed. “You’re funny. I’ve got until two days after prom to figure this out. I don’t know the plan, but I do know this: my playing days are over.”

“Okay. Whatever you choose, just make sure it’s really what you want." Malia hesitated for a moment, her eyes flicking to the side. She hadn’t expected him to say it like that—to want to follow her. It sounded flattering, but also … complicated. Did she want him there because it was what he truly wanted, or because he didn’t know where else to go?

A knot formed in her stomach, but she pushed it down. Now wasn’t the time to say more. Not yet. *Not because you lost the game. Or because you’re mad. Or frustrated. Think it through, Dillion.*

Dillion turned over on the bed and stared at the ceiling. He pulled out his phone, slid in his headphones, and played his favorite playlist. The opening notes of Meek Mills’s "What’s free" filled his ears: melancholy, familiar. It matched the swirl of emotions inside him: loss, clarity, and a strange sense of freedom. For the first time in his life, he wasn’t following anyone’s lead. He was content and starting to believe this could be his moment.

Chapter 7: Cradling

In lacrosse, cradling is carrying the ball in the stick and securing it. On the night of prom, Dillion finds himself at a crossroads between the boy shaped by his father's expectations and the young man searching for his own truth. As laughter and lights fill the evening, deeper questions surface about identity, legacy, and what it means to choose your own path. With Malia by his side, Dillion begins to confront the silence at home and the uncertainty within himself—realizing that some rides don't end when the whistle blows, and some dreams are only real when they're yours to chase.

It was prom night, and instead of cleats and turf, there were polished shoes, limousines, and bowties. The families gathered at Malia's house, where her mother had transformed the living room into a staging area of finger foods, sparkling cider, and soft jazz playing in the background. Dillion's mom and Layla worked together on makeup and hair, beaming with maternal pride. It was a celebration of endings and new beginnings.

Across town, Dillion laid out his garments on the bed like a soldier inspecting his armor. Every piece had a place, every fold, a memory. He rehearsed how the woman at the suit shop had explained the bowtie—his mother's choice. His father, once the king of game-day rituals, was now a ghost in the basement. Dillion hadn't heard more than footsteps from him in days.

Alex, already dressed, lounged in the corner. The two friends—polar opposites—shared space but not the same outlook.

"Where's your dad?" Alex asked, his blond curls hanging behind the chair like ivy.

"Downstairs somewhere," Dillion muttered, only half believing it himself.

The conversation that followed peeled back layers that neither had shared before. Alex, always perceived as lucky—birthday Lexuses, lavish parties, perfect grades—revealed a different reality: disconnected parents, performative affection, and a life curated for show.

Dillion, quiet through most of it, asked the question that had been eating at him all year.

“Are you happy?”

Alex didn’t understand. He lived in the moment. He never thought about purpose.

But Dillion did. Purpose had always been his North Star, first given to him in a lacrosse stick by his father, nurtured by years of drills and discipline. Now, with college looming and his passion uncertain, Dillion wondered if the game was his or just something handed down to him. Was lacrosse his dream or just the vessel of his father’s hopes?

And where was his father now? That thought lingered as he dressed. For every polished shoe and buttoned cuff, there was a question. Why am I mad at him? Did he only want what was best for me, or did he just not know how to show up in other ways?

“Bro, we gotta go! My mom needs sunlight for the pictures!” Alex called.

They stomped downstairs, but Dillion paused, just for a second. The cracked basement door was quiet. He looked for signs, even just the sound of feet shuffling upstairs. Nothing. Only the faint murmur of a TV.

He stepped outside, the trim on the house duller now, the lawn slightly overgrown. His father used to take pride in every corner of this yard. "God gave us the earth to manage," he'd say, "this little patch of heaven." But now it was fading, just like their connection.

Across the street, the limo shimmered, and his mother, camera in hand, called to them like a director of a coming-of-age film. Malia's house buzzed with excitement. Layla guarded the front door like a castle gate, hiding the royal court within.

"Where's Dad?" Dillion asked his mom as she snapped photos relentlessly.

"I don't know, baby," she said, lowering the lens. "Just give him time. Tonight's a big night. Let's enjoy it."

And then came the procession. The girls emerged one by one, pageant-like in poise and grace. But it was Malia who stole Dillion's breath. She wasn't just a friend tonight; she was radiant. Her hair shimmered with soft lights, her dress moved like starlight, and for a moment, Dillion couldn't remember the last time he saw her as just Malia.

"Where's my best friend?" he asked as she approached.

"The same place mine is," she answered, teasing him with a smirk.

They posed for photos. The moms wept. The limo swallowed them whole.

Inside, the ride was filled with chatter, music, and laughter; but Dillion drifted inward. As the city moved past the tinted windows, he thought again of lacrosse. The ride. The pursuit. The moment after losing the ball and deciding to fight for it back. That was where he'd always lived.

Tonight was no different. It wasn't just prom; it was Dillion realizing he was still in the ride, but maybe now, he had to choose what he was chasing.

As the lights of Sammy's Trattoria drew close, searchlights dancing in the sky, he turned to Malia.

Malia led their group to the entrance of the restaurant where two parent volunteers checked tickets for entry. The soft lighting of the gave everything a warm, golden glow.

"Hello, Mrs. Witherspoon," Malia said brightly.

The woman, banana-colored eyeshadow glittering under the lights, gave her a once-over and beamed. "Malia, don't you clean up well." She looked at Dillion and grinned. "And who is this handsome young man? Your boyfriend?"

"He wishes," Malia said with a teasing smirk. "This is my best friend. We've known each other forever."

"Well, that's how it all starts, baby." Mrs. Witherspoon winked and handed over their table assignments. "Y'all have a good time now."

As they stepped further inside, Dillion glanced around at the clusters of students. "So, where are all your hot friends? All I see are nerds in dresses."

Malia shot him a sharp look. "You're such a chauvinist sometimes, you know that?"

"I'm just saying, that's seventy-five percent of the reason I said yes to this thing."

"And the other twenty-five?"

"I heard the words *free* and *limo*. That was enough."

They entered the banquet room to a blend of excited voices and soft 90s boy band tracks playing through the speakers. The ambiance was nostalgic and whimsical.

"Is this a 90s-themed party?" Dillion cupped his hands around his ears like an old man.

"Student government wanted the full theme," Malia explained, "but we compromised—90s music only. Everything else is modern."

"You know I'm turning up when Backstreet Boys drop. That's Mom's jam."

"I know," Malia laughed, "and I also know you can't dance."

"What? I *can* cut some rug." Dillion stepped ahead and started pumping his hands wildly in the air, hips thrusting to imaginary music.

Malia raised an eyebrow. "Yeah, just like I said—no rhythm. That's gotta be your white side."

"Don't take it there. Last time you danced, I thought you were having a seizure. I almost gave you CPR."

"Whatever," she said with a grin. "Our table's near the stage."

The banquet stage shimmered with rope lights, balloon arches standing guard on either side. It felt like a teen dream dipped in neon.

"I'm glad we came," Dillion said as they settled in. The dim lighting caught the glitter dusted across Malia's cheeks, and he couldn't help but stare a moment longer than usual. "I needed a change of pace."

"Yeah. Me too. Everything's been … a lot lately."

"Graduation. Next steps. It's all been so heavy."

"Agreed," Malia nodded. "Now quit looking at me and go find your 'hot girls'."

They both laughed and left the table, wandering the venue's curious setup. It was no ordinary prom—part formal dance, part brainy amusement park. Interactive exhibits and oddball installations encouraged students to explore like kids again.

"This is silly," Malia said, hopping into a pit filled with baseball-sized plastic balls, "but it's fun."

"Let's see what's up there." Dillion pointed to a spiral staircase in the corner of the room.

"It's getting late. Shouldn't we go back inside?"

"Don't be a prude. Let's live a little. This place is awesome."

They weaved past clusters of people and began their quiet ascent. The metal stairs spiraled toward the glass ceiling above, higher than expected. At the top, a landing led to a door—unlocked—and beyond it, the rooftop.

"Let's go!"

"Really, Dillion? In these heels? Is that gravel?"

"Take them off. Come on, live in the moment."

With a sigh, Malia slipped off her shoes and followed him outside. The city stretched before them, a tapestry of light. Towering buildings twinkled like ornaments, and the harbor glimmered in the distance, still and peaceful. Above them, the stars blinked into view, scattered across the sky like sequins on velvet.

Dillion removed his suit jacket and draped it around Malia's shoulders. The breeze teased at her curls as she clutched the lapels.

"This is incredible," she whispered. "You don't see the city like this from the ground. Just traffic and trash and people glued to their phones."

"Up here," Dillion said softly, "it feels like we're the only ones alive."

Malia reached into the pocket of the jacket. "I left my phone in the limo. Do you have yours? I want a picture."

Dillion patted his pants. "Nope. Empty. Maybe it fell out when I gave you my jacket."

"No big deal. Let's just sit a while."

They found a raised ledge a few feet from the building's edge and sat side by side. The air was quiet, cool, and alive.

"Just think, this is it," Malia said. "After this year, we're on our own. College. It still sounds weird."

"Yeah. And I still don't know what I'm supposed to do."

"Do what feels right. Follow your heart."

"I don't have a heart to follow; that's the problem. I've never had space to figure out what I actually wanted."

"Never?"

"I always did what was expected. That just became my normal."

He paused, watching the stars. "Remember in fifth grade when we had to choose an instrument?"

"You picked the saxophone. I picked the clarinet. We were the woodwind dream team."

"I loved it creating music, it came from me. It was mine."

"So, why'd you stop?"

"I was good. Really good. My teacher emailed my dad and asked if I could take after-school lessons."

"That's awesome! I didn't know that."

Dillion smiled faintly. "I told my dad I loved it more than lacrosse. I wanted to play professionally."

Malia turned to him slowly. "And?"

"He told me saxophones were for street performers. Said it'd get me nowhere. He took my sax and emailed the teacher back, said I wasn't interested anymore."

"Wait—what? Are you serious?"

"I was embarrassed. I thought maybe he was right. Maybe I wasn't that good. But now I think I was. I think he just didn't want anything interfering with lacrosse."

Malia said nothing. She just looked at him—really looked at him—and a tear rolled silently down her cheek.

Dillion noticed. "What? Why are you crying? That was years ago."

"It's not about the saxophone," she said, brushing the tear away. "It's about him taking something from you that you loved. Something that was yours."

He didn't respond. He just looked back at the stars, his jaw tight.

The moonlight caught the flecks of glitter on Malia's cheeks. She looked ethereal, otherworldly. And for a long, quiet moment, neither of them spoke.

They just sat together, high above the world, holding the silence like a sacred thing.

"I'm starting to see you're finally beginning to really contemplate a lot of things you've held in all these years. Is this because of the game you lost?" Malia asked softly.

"I think it's everything," Dillion replied, still gazing at the moon. "I just feel like I don't know who I am, because no one ever let me figure it out. Is it my fault? Dad's? I don't know. But I made a promise to myself: from now on, what I do will be *my* decision and no one else's. Do you feel like your life is your own?"

"Well ... who's to say what's right or wrong?" Malia said, thoughtful. "I think our parents just want the best for us. They don't have a crystal ball. They learn from their past and project what they think is best onto us."

"So, when do we say, 'Thanks for the guidance, but I've got it from here'?"

"I think it's different for everyone. Every family's different, Dillion."

"Well, I just want to do things my way. And however it goes, I can say I did it on *my* terms."

Time grew late. From below, they heard faint yelling and laughter. Malia looked over the ledge of the pavilion.

"Dillion, I think people are leaving! What time is it?"

"I don't have my phone," he said.

Both leapt to their feet and ran to the rooftop door that led to the staircase.

"It's locked!" Dillion tugged at it with all his strength.

"What now?" Malia said, trying to help him with the little bit of handle left.

Dillion ran to the edge of the building.

"Helloooo! Hello!" he shouted, waving his arms wildly. The only response was the sound of music and laughter from the cars driving off below.

"I'm sure Alex won't leave us; we came with him."

"Maybe they think we left early."

"I hope not…"

"What are we going to do? Nobody can hear us up here."

"There's nothing we *can* do but wait, unless you've got a Bat-Signal to light up."

They found comfort near a partially raised ledge in the middle of the roof and sat down.

"It could be worse, I guess," Malia said.

"Like what?"

"I don't know, but that's what people say when things aren't great."

They laughed, knowing they always found a way to stay grounded when they were together.

Suddenly, a voice cut through the silence. "Hey! What are you kids doing out here?"

"Yes!" Dillion jumped up.

"Thank you! We got locked out!" Malia ran toward the man in blue overalls and a backwards Ravens hat.

"You're lucky I came out for a smoke—no one ever comes up here," said Sammy.

"Has everyone left?" Dillion asked, out of breath.

"Yeah, just the cleanup crew is left now."

They hurried downstairs, passing Sammy as he lit a cigarette. The banquet hall was empty. The parking lot too.

"We were up there *that* long?" Malia asked, stunned.

"This is crazy. Do you know anyone's number? I don't have any memorized."

"If we can find a phone, I know my mom's."

"Let's just get an Uber."

"You need a phone and app. We've got neither."

“Maybe one of the crew can help.”

They found someone willing to lend them a phone.

“I’ll call my mom, she’ll come,” Malia said. After a few rings, she shook her head. “She’s not answering. Try your mom.”

Dillion took the phone, dialed, and listened. Nothing.

“Let me try one more number,” he punched in digits slowly. The line rang, then connected.

“Hey … can you pick us up? It’s a long story, but we need a ride.”

There was a long pause.

“Well, can you at least get us a cab or an Uber?”

There was another pause.

“Okay,” Dillion said, just before the phone died.

“What’s going on?” Malia asked.

“Dad’s coming to get us.”

“Is he mad?”

“Yep.”

“Why not just send an Uber?”

“He said he’s around the corner, and he’s not spending another dime on this prom,” Dillion muttered as he plopped onto the curb. Malia joined him.

After a long wait, Dillion's father's cherry-red SUV pulled up, a bit more weathered now, but unmistakable. The window rolled down.

“So, can you explain how you two are here and your limo and cell phones are across the city?” his dad asked coldly.

Before they could rise fully, his hands were gripping the wheel like he was trying to break it. The silence was heavy. Dillion and Malia approached the car, waiting for the locks to click.

“It’s a long story, Dad,” Dillion said, trying the door.

“I’ve got time. It’s a long drive home.”

He finally unlocked the door. Malia climbed in cautiously, her tone bright and strained. “Hi! Thanks for coming to get us.”

Dillion slid in beside her. She sat in the middle, between them.

“We got lost, ended up on the roof, the door locked behind us, the owner found us, then we called you,” Dillion said in one breath.

His father stared at them in the rearview mirror.

“I guess that answers my question,” he said, then turned up the radio slightly.

“That’s it?” Dillion asked.

“What do you mean? If that’s what happened, that’s what happened.”

“You didn’t talk to me all day. You didn’t even see me off to prom. And that’s all you have to say?”

"I left a note. I thought I'd be back before you left, but I lost track of time. I had some things I needed to work out."

"You could've at least called Mom."

"I *did* call. I texted too. Since you didn't have your phone, that explains a lot now, doesn't it?"

Dillion deflated.

"So what's up with you hiding in the basement?" he asked quietly. "Why now?"

"I'm sorry, Dillion. I really am. I've been doing some soul-searching. I realized how you feel about me is exactly how I felt about *my* dad. I wanted to guide you along your way. He gave me nothing. No help. No direction. And I promised I'd never do that to my own kid."

He paused.

"But in trying to help, I forced my goals on you. That wasn't right. I thought I was bringing us closer, but I was pushing you away. I see that now."

"I don't see what your father has to do with any of this."

"I didn't either. But I kept asking myself, *what if someone had just shown me a path?* Maybe I'd be better off. But now I know: a path isn't something you can hand someone. It's something they have to *choose*."

Malia stayed silent. She could feel the emotional weight between the two of them. This was the first real heart-to-heart they'd ever had.

“I just want you to grow into the man *you* want to be,” his father said. “Your mom and I—we’ve given you the tools. Now it’s up to you. If you’re making informed choices that make you happy, I can live with that.”

Dillion didn’t know what to say. He’d waited his whole life to hear those words, that his father believed in him.

Just then, headlights grew brighter in the windshield—too bright, too fast.

“Dad, watch out! Is that car drifting into our lane—?!”

Dillion had no time to react.

The headlights surged forward, growing so blindingly bright that the world outside vanished into white. Malia clutched his shoulders, her arms wrapped around him in a desperate, protective grip.

The car jolted violently. Dillion's father had swerved—instinctively, selflessly—putting the driver’s side in direct line with the oncoming vehicle.

“Hold on!” he shouted, voice raw with urgency.

And then, the light swallowed everything. A searing white engulfed the interior of the car. Time fractured. Silence.

Chapter 8: Intermission

Halftime in lacrosse is a pause—a chance to regroup, refocus, and face the truth. For Dillion, this was his intermission. Broken, dazed, and unsure if he could still play—let alone what the score was.

Dillion awoke to a blur of white light—still blinding, but softer now. He could hear mechanical beeps as his eyes fought off the sting of blurred vision. His head was spinning. Voices murmured near him, indistinct. His eyes burned like hot coal as he forced them open. The haze slowly gave way to sharper sounds and clarity. Inside his mind, a desperate scream: *Dad! Malia! Where am I?* The only sounds he could make were the ones echoing inside his head. He tried to move; to feel his legs. Nothing. He could only hear.

"Dillion, if you can hear me, just relax. Rest," a soft voice whispered. A gentle pressure on his shoulder followed.

The voice was familiar, but distorted, like it came through cups of water held to his ears. He obeyed. He had no choice. His body was numb, and only the burning in his eyes grounded him in the moment.

"You're going to be okay. Besides some bumps and bruises, you'll be fine. You have a concussion, and your eyes are swollen from the impact of the accident. I'll let your mother know. She's been so worried. Just rest for now. I'll be back."

Dillion lay still, thoughts racing: *What happened? An accident?* He could remember the light, the crash, then nothing. Now, this.

Where's Dad? Where's Malia? he screamed silently.

No reply. Only the beeping machines and distant chatter answered.

"Can you hear me?" a voice emerged from the background.

It sounded familiar, but heavier, weighted with emotion.

"Dillion," again.

He tried to move his mouth. Nothing. But he knew that voice; it was Malia. Her tone was strained, burdened.

"The nurse just told us you were waking up. I just wanted to see if you could talk yet."

Dillion strained, and a low grunt escaped his throat.

"I knew you could hear me. They must've given you some strong stuff. Well, if you can hear me, the doctor said you'll be okay. You're just really swollen. He said because you're in such good shape, you withstood the crash really well. You wrapped yourself around me and absorbed most of the impact. I just have a few cuts from the glass."

Her words warmed him, then froze him. *What about Dad?*

He grunted again, more intensely. His body tensed. Malia heard the sound and grew silent.

Another grunt. Louder.

Malia understood. She couldn't answer. She collapsed to her knees beside his bed and wept.

All Dillion could hear now was Malia sobbing and the relentless beeping of machines. Her cries turned into pleas.

"No, no, no. I'm sorry, Dillion."

The medicine ran its course, and the burning in his eyes dulled. He could feel a tingle return to his fingertips. With effort, he moved his fingers, grasped the bedrail, and pulled himself upright. His right hand lifted the cover from his eyes. He looked down.

Malia knelt on the floor, fists against the ground, head bowed.

"Malia," he croaked.

She looked up, eyes swollen and red. Cuts from the glass scattered across her cheeks. She looked older, weathered.

"Where is Dad?" His voice was stronger now. He swung his legs off the bed, the cold linoleum shocking his feet. His hospital gown barely protected him from the chill.

"Dad. Where is he, Malia?"

She bowed her head and sat in the hard plastic chair with the faded floral print. Her hands trembled. Her lips quivered.

"Malia!" he demanded.

She stared ahead, through the room, past reality. Her mind had already accepted the truth.

Dillion stood, bracing against the bed, staggering toward the door.

"Sir, you need to get back to your bed," a stern voice said as gentle arms caught him.

"I'm looking for my father," he murmured, straining against the supportive hold.

"Sir, let's get you back into your room. I'll get you everything you need."

"I just need my father!" Dillion shouted.

Suddenly, he found himself surrounded and ushered back to bed. His body betrayed him; the strength had vanished. He slumped into the mattress. Malia remained seated, face buried in her hands.

"Sir, just lay down. We'll have someone come speak with you," an older male voice offered.

Then, his mother entered. Her hand covered her mouth, eyes wide with grief. Dillion looked up.

"Mom!"

She crossed the room, climbed into bed with him, and wrapped her arms around him as if holding a newborn. She sobbed into the pillow beneath his head. No words. Only the sound of tears falling.

Dillion stared at the ceiling lights, the same blinding brightness. He went numb. Tears streamed down his face. He clutched his mother. He didn't want to cry, but the tears found their way.

He remembered being a boy in this hospital. He hadn't understood back then. Now he was the one fate had chosen. He turned his head and met Malia's eyes.

She came over, and together, they huddled—Dillion, his mother, and Malia.

Through gasping sobs, Malia whispered, "He was in the same room as Nana."

Dillion understood. This was not just about now. This was a return to a pain they thought they'd buried. Death had returned.

Days passed. Dillion did the hardest thing he ever had to do—cremate his father. He placed the ashes into two necklaces: one for his mother, and one for himself.

His father had always said, "You're my heart. I always want to be close to yours."

His death shocked the family and the community. Colleagues, students he coached, and classmates came to show support. The wake overflowed with love, condolences, and donations.

But for Dillion's mother, the days shrank into darkness. She abandoned her bright editing studio upstairs and retreated into the basement, his father's memory cave. She watched old family videos and sifted through boxes, reliving simpler times.

Dillion, in those first days, handled the will and affairs. His father had planned well. The life insurance policy went to Dillion, the home and benefits to his mother. Dillion ensured every document was signed, every account settled.

Still, his mother stayed in the basement, eating only when Dillion brought her favorite meals.

"Mom, you need to eat," he said gently.

"I'm not hungry," she murmured, watching a home video of Dillion riding his bike. Her voice echoed faintly behind the recording: *Catch him!*

"He never did catch you," she said softly. "He always said you needed to fall. That's how you learn to stand up. I guess he did a good job. You're the strong one."

Dillion sat beside her, noticing the cup in her hand.

"Mom, what's in that cup?" he asked, spotting an empty bottle nearby.

"Something I found in your father's drawer," she said, raising the glass to her lips.

"You never drink. Don't start now," he said, reaching gently.

"I've never felt so alone either." She clutched the cup closer.

He pulled back. She wasn't ready to let go.

"If it wasn't for you, I don't think your dad would've stayed with me."

"That's not true. He loved you."

"I think he learned to love me—or tolerated me for the greater good."

"Mom, I don't think this is fair to Dad right now. You need rest."

Dillion walked to the wet bar, filled a glass of water, and set it beside her. He caressed her head gently. Tears slid down her face. He knew: if he didn't help to pull her out of this darkness, he would lose her too.

He pulled out his phone, scrolled to Malia's mom's contact, and typed: **"Come over ASAP."** No reply.

Moments later, he heard the creak of the door upstairs. Light footsteps came down the steps.

"Hello?" a familiar, gentle voice called.

"Hey. We're in here," Dillion replied.

Malia's mother descended, carrying a warm dish—his mother's favorite: stuffed shells and garlic bread. The scent filled the air. Dillion's stomach growled.

"You guys hungry?" she asked as she placed the food on the table, cutting through the staleness of alcohol and old tears.

"That smells amazing," Dillion said, gesturing toward the plates already set out for his mother from the previous days.

Just as he got up to grab a plate, his phone lit up. He looked at the caller ID—Coach.

"Hey, Coach," Dillion answered, walking up the basement stairs to get a better signal. The basement rarely had any reception; he was surprised the call even came through.

"Got a minute?" Coach asked firmly, but not in a cold manner.

"Yeah. Sure."

"I know you've got a lot going on, but I wanted to talk to you about your future, Dillion."

"Okay."

"What are your plans? Do you still want to play lacrosse?"

"I haven't really thought about it lately, Coach."

"I understand. Look, I spoke with your father before he passed. He wanted me to reach out for one last conversation, one last push. I'm calling because I promised him I would."

Dillion's throat tightened. "Umm... okay."

"I talked to Georgetown. They still want you. A lot of schools did, but most of the scholarship spots are gone. Georgetown's willing to work out a late admission. Your dad really wanted me to help make that happen."

"With all due respect, Coach, I don't think leaving my mom right now is a good idea."

"I get that. I really do. But I promised your father I'd have this talk with you. Just think about it. Georgetown is still open to working something out. How are you feeling physically?"

"I'm okay. I feel fine."

"Good. But this opportunity won't last forever, Dillion. This is your life. Think it over. I'll have the coach reach out to you soon."

"Alright. I will, Coach." Dillion stared at his phone screen which had cracked during the accident. Another reminder.

"I'll be in touch."

The line went dead. Dillion stuffed his phone into his pocket and gathered his things.

"I'm going down the street!" he yelled down the basement stairs. No reply. It was probably for the best. His mother needed time and space to process everything. He suspected the death of his father unearthed feelings she'd long buried—some she feared, some she simply never dared say. Their marriage, though good on the surface, suddenly felt more fragile than he'd ever noticed. Was this just grief talking or had silence stretched too far in their home?

Still, they had a good life. He was living proof.

He stepped out into the warm evening and made his way to Malia's.

"Malia!" he shouted as he unlocked the front door with his usual key.

"Yo! I'm in here!" she called out, voice light with relief.

He found her in her computer chair. Without a word, he flopped onto her bed, staring up at the stucco ceiling and breathing deeply. Just being out of the house felt like fresh air for his soul.

"What's on your mind now, le Poète?"

"Who?"

"The Thinker. You know, the statue?"

"You're such a nerd," he said, cracking a small smile.

"You're just jealous. Did you see my mom?"

"Yeah, she's at my house now."

"That's good. How's your mom holding up?"

"She's ... seen better days."

"Anything I can do?"

"Just time. And your mom being there might help."

"I'm sorry, Dillion. All of this is still so surreal."

"I'm starting to wrap my head around it. Coach called today."

"About what?"

“My dad. Apparently, before he died, he asked Coach to reach out about Georgetown. He still wanted me to play.”

“What are you going to do?”

“I don’t know. It’s weird knowing that was one of his last conversations—about me, about this.”

“Well, what do *you* want?”

“My plans took a huge detour. My mom’s a mess. I don’t know if I can leave her. I feel lost. But maybe this is what he worked for. Maybe I should go. Should I talk to Mom?”

“Is she ready for that conversation?”

“I just don’t want to leave her like this.”

“Either way, you have to do what’s best for *you*, Dillion—not just for your dad, not even for your mom. For you.”

“I know that sounds right, Malia, but what if my father died believing in something, and I just let it go? What if we all sacrificed for nothing?”

“It’s not nothing,” she said softly. “And it’s not the end of the world either way. Talk to the coach. See how it feels. You don’t have to decide everything today.”

He looked up at the ceiling again, silent.

Maybe his dad had it right all along. Maybe Georgetown was the path.

Chapter 9: Georgetown

Georgetown, the oldest Catholic university in America, had long been a place where history met ambition. Its lacrosse field was no exception—home to legends, rivalries, and relentless grit. Now Dillion stood among them. The past didn't guarantee a future here. He'd have to earn it: one sprint, one rep, one play at a time.

"Sooo, how's the training going?" asked Malia.

"It's conditioning—and it's kicking my butt. I'm sore every day, but it's all good," Dillion replied.

"I guess that's the name of the game, huh? No pain, no gain. Where are you staying on campus now?"

"They've got me in Village A. It's pretty nice; a good view of the Potomac. There's an overlook, and at night all the kids come out and hang there. It's different, especially being in the city."

"You're a city guy at heart," Malia chuckled.

"When are you coming to visit?"

"Well, my classes are pretty demanding, but I'll figure out a weekend soon. College Park isn't far from you. Your mom coming up anytime?"

"She hasn't picked up the phone today. Can you call your mom and have her check on her?"

"Yeah, sure. I'll text her when we get off the phone."

"Okay, I'll hit you later."

"Ciao."

Dillion sat back in his rollaway chair, gazing out of the massive picture window that spanned the front wall of his dorm. The day had brought him a strange sense of release. The team was welcoming, but he was one of the smallest guys on the squad. He knew he'd have to grind harder than ever just to be considered for playing time.

The Georgetown lacrosse team was stacked with athletic specimens from elite programs. Top recruits, just like him. The only difference was, they had college experience. He didn't. Not yet. This was going to be the most demanding culture he'd ever been a part of, and he knew it. To compete, to even be noticed, he'd have to outwork everyone.

Starting school and joining the conditioning program all at once was overwhelming. With the added weight of his father's death and the constant worry for his mother, Dillion knew he wasn't in top competitive shape for fall lacrosse. He had always been the best in his class. Now, he was surrounded by guys he used to follow on Instagram and watch in highlight reels. They were teammates now. Brothers in battle. But they had something he didn't: time ... experience ... balance.

Academics came first. He needed to lock in his study routine. If he didn't get that down now, there'd be no lacrosse later. What kept his head from spinning off his shoulders were the daily calls from Malia, her voice a reminder that no matter what, someone was in his corner. Chance had brought them together, and destiny had bonded them. He'd do anything for her, and he knew she would do the same.

He got up and paced the dorm suite. Sharing a living space with strangers was unusual. Each guy had different habits, backgrounds, and outlooks. Still, it was a new frontier, and the constant presence of people kept him from dwelling on the past. On his dad. On Malia being far away.

Maybe this distance was necessary to force him into something new. A new chapter. A new version of himself. Still, lacrosse remained his anchor. The game brought him back to what he loved most: competing, pushing, and achieving.

Dillion stayed in a dorm suite which was divided into a quad: two rooms on each side, two guys per room. His room was tight, half the size of bedroom back home. The beds were wooden platforms raised high for storage. The walls were thick cinder blocks, painted over enough times to feel almost soft. Each quad had a shared bathroom with four stalls and two showers. Just as Dillion turned on the water to hop in the shower, in entered his roommate—Isaac.

Isaac was a local guy, studying foreign government, and manager of the girls' volleyball team. He was short, stocky, and had a vaguely Native American look, though it seemed diluted through generations. Dillion thought about asking but chose not to. Isaac had that unmistakable prep-school vibe—polos, khakis, brands like Vineyard Vines and Patagonia hanging neatly on his bed, ready for the closet.

"Hey, man," Isaac said, passing by. "My mom baked a ton of chocolate chip and sugar cookies. Help yourself. They're in the Pyrex on the bed."

"Cool," Dillion replied, checking the water temp. "Trying to cut sugar right now, but I might grab one. Thanks."

"I feel you, bro. I need to drop some pounds too. Gotta get sexy for the upperclassmen. New year, new me! Should've started this summer, but senior week lasted all summer." He laughed, yelling through the cracked door as Dillion stepped into the shower.

Afterward, Dillion dried off and walked back into their room in a robe and shower shoes, grabbing fresh clothes and returning to the bathroom to change. Sharing a room wasn't the weird part, it was the close quarters. That would take getting used to.

"So you're on the lacrosse team?" Isaac asked, hanging up clothes in the cramped closet.

"Yeah." Dillion pulled out a workout shirt from his duffel.

"Wait—are you *the* Dillion Frank? From François Garçon?"

"I guess. I went there the last four years."

"Dude. You were *kind of* a big deal. I managed my high school's lacrosse team, and my guys talked about you all the time."

"Wrong guy then," Dillion said with a half-smile.

"They said you were the best but didn't commit to any universities. Didn't even take official visits. Man, if I had offers like that, I'd have gone everywhere—been treated like royalty. Why Georgetown? You could've gone anywhere."

"It's complicated."

"Yeah … they talked about you having a breakdown after the championship. Then your dad passing away. That's rough."

"I don't really want to talk about that."

"Totally. Sorry. I'm just kind of shocked you're my roommate. I gotta post this … I'm heading to the café before it closes. You wanna roll?"

Dillion looked at the half-eaten bagel on his desk. His stomach grumbled. He needed something better—pasta, bananas, water. Recovery food. His dad always said that mattered most.

"Sure," Dillion said, tossing his sweaty clothes in the hamper.

Chapter 10: The Alley

In lacrosse, "the alley" is the narrow lane along the sidelines—tight, fast, and risky. It's where bold players go one-on-one, knowing there's little room to escape and even less to hide. For Dillion, this chapter was his alley: unexpected, intimate, and just risky enough to feel real. Meeting Rebecca wasn't part of the game plan, but sometimes the best plays happen when you take the lane anyway.

The cafeteria was packed with athletes grabbing food before closing—soccer, football, basketball, even club teams. Dillion could spot them. Athletes had a look.

"I'm gonna find my cousin real quick. Save us a table?" Isaac said, dropping his bookbag at a table in the back.

Dillion went through the line and chose pasta, bananas, and three bottles of water. Simple, focused fuel. He sat where Isaac had left the bag, as steam from the pasta warming his face. His stomach roared. He dove in.

"Slow down, bro. Pretty sure there's more left," a voice joked.

Dillion looked up—and froze.

"This is my cousin, Rebecca. Sorry it took so long; she was socializing." Isaac said.

Rebecca was stunning. Tall—6'1". Her long blonde hair was streaked with silver. Her features were soft and angelic, like she stepped out of a magazine. Dillion couldn't even register her words at first.

"You've got sauce on your chin," she teased, pointing.

"Hello? You good, Dillion?" Isaac waved a hand in front of his face.

“Yeah. Just tired. Long day.”

As they talked, Dillion found himself mesmerized. Rebecca had a glow, a quiet confidence. And she was sharp. Their conversation drifted into social politics, her work on campus, and eventually, his lacrosse career.

“So, what made you come to Georgetown?” she asked.

Isaac jumped in. “He’s on the lacrosse team!”

Rebecca raised a brow. “Why aren’t you with the team, then? They’re like a frat here.”

“He’s Dillion Frank,” Isaac added. “His name was everywhere last year.”

“I think I’ve heard that name. Did you play at Garçon?”

“Yeah,” Dillion said, surprised he spoke at all.

“What made you come here?” she asked again, genuinely.

“My father,” Dillion said, eyes dropping to the uneaten fruit.

“Is he an alum?”

“No. First to attend. He was just a fan.”

“Is he ... not a fan anymore?”

“He passed away this summer. Car accident.”

Rebecca paused. “I’m so sorry.”

“It’s okay. I’m adjusting.”

They changed the subject. Rebecca was a former lacrosse player; a knee injury ended her freshman season.

That caught Dillion off guard. “You? You don’t look like you’d want to get dirty.”

“She played *here,*” Isaac said. “Freshman year.”

Rebecca laughed. “That was a former life. Now it’s planning events, running meetings, networking.”

Eventually, she had to leave. “Nice meeting you, Dillion.”

“You, too. See you around.”

Dillion barely touched his food after that. Isaac, oblivious, grinned.

“Let me guess, you’ve got a crush on my cousin.”

“No. She’s cool. Not my type.”

“She’s everyone’s type, bro. *She’s my type,* and she’s my cousin!”

Water shot from Dillion’s nose as they both laughed.

Back at the dorm as they climbed the stairs, Isaac rambled about local parties. Dillion half-listened. His mind was still with Rebecca. He replayed their conversation. What he said. What he should’ve said. Her laugh. Her presence. He hadn’t felt this way before—this electricity. The only thing he could comparison he could think of was the night before Christmas as a kid. That tingling anticipation, excitement and nerves in equal measure.

As they reached the door, Dillion’s phone buzzed. The screen lit up: Malia.

Just like that, his thoughts shifted.

He answered. “Hello?”

“Hey! I’ve been waiting for your call. What are you doing?”

“Just finished eating,” he said. “Hanging with my roommate.”

Dillion stood in the hallway, angling his phone just enough to shield it from Isaac’s view. His friend leaned against the wall, raising an eyebrow and mouthing something exaggeratedly.

"Is that your girlfriend?" Isaac mouthed.

Dillion rolled his eyes and turned the camera closer to his face.

"This is my best friend," he said loudly, as much for Isaac’s benefit as Malia’s.

"Who are you talking to?" Malia asked on the other end of the line, her voice confused and slightly amused.

Dillion walked away from the dorm door toward the side of the building where a stool sat next to a vending machine. He dropped down onto it with a sigh.

“I’ll be in in a minute,” he called out to Isaac. “Just leave the door open. I left my keys inside.”

Isaac shrugged and disappeared.

“So, what are you guys up to?” Malia asked, as she settled into her own routine hundreds of miles away.

“Nothing major. Just hanging out. I’m about to look over some new plays before bed. Long day.”

"Same. Some girls invited me to check out this sorority thing on campus," she said. "Thinking about going to a social just to see what it's like."

Dillion grinned. "School hasn't even started and they're already recruiting?"

"It's more like an academic society," she said. "A bunch of girls with shared interests, support systems and all that."

"So … a geek party?" he teased.

"Basically. Not everyone gets to be a gifted athlete like you," she shot back.

"I know," he sighed dramatically. "It's a real shame. The mold broke after me. So lonely up here at the top."

"Speaking of lonely…" Her voice softened. "You need to call your mom."

"I will. I'll text her before I go to sleep."

"Why don't you just call? I'm sure she wants to hear your voice."

"I will…" He hesitated. "Look, I've got some stuff to handle. Enjoy your honors party. I'll call you back."

"Okay. And hey—if you need to talk about anything, I'm here. I was there too, Dillion. I get it."

"Goodnight, Malia."

He ended the call and sat for a long moment, the screen still glowing in his hand. His thumb hovered over his mom's contact. He wanted to call her. He wanted to hear her voice, ask how she was doing, even just say goodnight. But he couldn't do it. Not tonight. Not with the weight of his father's absence still too fresh. Every conversation dug into the wound. Her grief was still raw, still unfiltered. And every time he heard it, it tore open something within him he was trying so hard to keep closed. If he stayed in that place, mentally and emotionally, he'd never be able to move forward. Never breathe fully again. He pocketed the phone and climbed into bed without another word, eyes wide open in the dark.

The alarm blared at 4:30 a.m., a sharp buzz that vibrated through his skull. Dillion sat up, bleary-eyed but awake. He threw on his Georgetown sweats over yesterday's gear, splashed cold water on his face, brushed his teeth, and slipped quietly through the dorm room, careful not to wake Isaac, who snored like a malfunctioning chainsaw.

Outside, the campus was still cloaked in darkness. Players emerged from dorms and townhouses like shadows, hoodies pulled tight, their steps slow and heavy. No one slept much.

Inside the locker room, Coach Yarling stood on a makeshift wooden platform like a general surveying his troops.

"Harper!" he barked.

"Here, sir!" a voice responded.

"Malloy!"

"Present!"

"Canter!"

"Sir!"

"Dillion Frank!"

"Here!"

Coach Yarling squinted at him. "Boy, what's your last name? Dillion or Frank? You got two first names."

"Frank, sir."

"I was told never to trust a man with two first names. Can I trust you?"

"Yes, sir."

Laughter rippled through the room.

"I'm Pete Yarling, your new best friend," he said. "Some of you prima donnas already know me. I've been strength and conditioning coach here for four years, but I've been doing this for twenty. You're my clay. I'm the sculptor. I don't play lacrosse, but I know performance science. Believe in the process."

He scanned the players, eyes narrowing like a hawk circling its prey.

"This week, we run. Then we run again. And when you think you're done? We run some more. Take off the sweats. No headphones. This ain't Pilates. This ain't hot yoga. This is real work."

He pointed toward the exit. "Ten minutes. Use the potty. Then meet me on the field. Long morning ahead."

The team stretched in a circle on the field. Tim and Lathan led the warm-up. Yarling paced like a lion.

"This field is sacred ground," he barked. "This is where we play. But today, we train. Training happens on the battlefield."

He paused.

"You'll start on Prospect Street. Run the Exorcist Steps. Cross the Key Bridge. Down M Street. Up 28th. Right on O. Over Wisconsin. Back onto O. Left on 37th. Then do it again."

A few players glanced around, worried.

"If you don't know your ABCs or numbers, find a buddy who does."

The players hit the streets. Dillion ran beside Tim and Lathan, determined not to fall behind. The Exorcist Steps loomed—narrow, steep, and endless. Tim did pull-ups on the railings as they waited for others.

"Pace yourselves," he warned.

They crossed the Key Bridge, the Potomac glistening below. Georgetown's skyline stretched behind them. It was beautiful and unforgiving.

By the time they hit M Street, the pack thinned. Dillion's legs burned. His lungs screamed. His vision blurred.

Running is mental, he told himself. *Running is mental...* Then, unexpectedly, he heard a voice.

"You look a little out of shape there."

He turned, startled. Rebecca leaned on the window of a bright yellow townhouse, a teasing smile on her face.

"You're almost there," she said. "Doing pretty good for a rookie."

He blinked. "How... how do you—"

"Straight down, left on 37th," she said, already turning away. "Coach'll be waiting."

Before he could respond, she was gone.

Fueled by something deeper than pride, Dillion surged forward. He pushed past the pain, past the doubt, past every voice in his head that told him he wasn't good enough. When he finally reached the field again, Coach Yarling didn't even look up from his clipboard.

"Good time, Frank—Dillion—whatever your name is."

Other players trickled in behind him.

"You're only as strong as your weakest player," the coach said without emotion. "You've got to do better."

Tim clapped Dillion on the back. "Good job, newbie."

Dillion bent over, hands on knees. "Thanks."

"First time I did that run," Tim said. "I couldn't even make it back across the bridge."

"Yeah. Good job," Lathan added. But the tone was flat. Measured.

Dillion caught the subtext—*you're not there yet.*

He skipped the locker room. His dorm was closer. He dragged himself up three flights of metal stairs, gripping the rail to keep from collapsing.

At the top, he reached for the doorknob just as it swung open. Isaac stood there, blinking at him.

“Dude,” he said, stepping back. “You look like death. Dude, you look like crap.”

“Issac, not right now.”

Dillion walked past Issac into the shower. He managed to crawl out of his sweat-soaked T-shirt and shorts, letting them fall into a wet heap on the tile floor. The face of the school mascot stared up from his shorts as he crutched over, under the hot spray. Steam filled the space, enveloping him, easing the pain in his lungs and his burning shins.

“Dude, I’m going to get breakfast. You need anything?” Issac yelled through the door.

“Yeah, just get me some fruit. I have water and protein here.”

“You got it, brother.”

Dillion let the steam open his airways. He felt better. His shins still burned, but he knew it would pass with time.

Issac returned shortly, fruit in hand.

“Here you go, bro. Eat up.”

“Thanks, bro. That’s clutch.”

“Yeah, heard you had a rough morning.”

“Heard? Who told you?”

“Rebecca called me laughing. Said she saw you when you stopped to catch your breath. She didn’t think it was you at first.”

“She called you?”

"Yeah. Said your roommate might need G.E.R.M.S."

"What's that?"

"Don't you remember anything from orientation? Georgetown Emergency Response Medical Services. Our campus ambulance." Issac chuckled.

"Oh. Right. Well, I can't think of anything right now. Pass me that water."

Issac grabbed the gallon of water from under Dillion's bed.

"She said you need real running shoes for asphalt. You're running with trail shoes; they're too stiff."

"Tell her thanks for the suggestion."

Dillion sprawled out on the bed, sipping the water, easing the fire in his lungs.

"I'm going to class. I'll be back around noon. Hopefully, you can make it to your classes today."

"I'll make it. Just need a baby nap. My first class is at 9 a.m. I'll be okay."

"Okay, brother. See you in a few."

Issac gathered his worn-out L.L. Bean backpack and left, the scent of his cologne lingering behind.

Silence settled over the room. Dillion welcomed it. He set his alarm, noticed two missed calls—one from Malia, one from Mom—and a text from Malia: *Hope you had a great workout. Call me when you can. Call your mother!*

Dillion leaned against the cinderblock wall that served as his headboard. He chose to rest instead of calling. It was going to be a long day. He slid his phone under his pillow, hoping the vibration would wake him in 45 minutes.

The phone's vibration woke him gently. His body ached, but his lungs felt clearer. The fruit Issac brought was mostly gone; only the apple remained. It would have to do.

He dressed in light sweats, grabbed his book bag, and remembered he had a book waiting at the Leavy Center. He needed to walk clear across campus to pick it up.

He noticed the TV was left on in the common room and the half-eaten food and Starbucks cups on the table. He hadn't spent much time with his roommates yet. He hoped to get to know them soon. College, for him, wasn't just about studying or lacrosse; it was a chance to grow, to meet people, to develop every aspect of himself.

He almost locked the door, then paused. What if one of the guys forgot their key? He left it unlocked—a dorm, after all, was still home.

The campus buzzed with life. Bookbags bounced against shoulders. It was officially back-to-school season. He made it to Leavy in time, picked up his book from the campus Barnes & Noble, and headed to math class—his strong suit, but always a challenge.

The lecture hall was massive and intimidating. The students, mostly prep types, looked like they'd stepped out of a J. Crew catalog. Dillion was accustomed to being one of the few students with olive skin and a background unconnected to Fortune 500 legacies. He was here to outwork everyone—not to prove he was better, but that he belonged. That hard work, grit, and focus mattered.

His father always said school required more than attendance. It required discipline, independent study, and a hunger for understanding. It wasn't always natural for Dillion, but when he struggled, Malia had always helped him. Now, there were no Malia. No Dad. Just him.

Just as he sat reflecting, Issac strolled in with a smirk and sat beside him.

"Bro, who sits front and center in math?"

"I hate math, but I've gotta get through it," Dillion replied.

"How are you with math?" Issac asked, sipping his watery drink.

"I'm okay, I guess. We'll find out. We can study together. If not, we can always drop it."

"Yeah, and you know who's a stud at math? Rebecca," Issac said pointedly.

"I think we'll be okay, Issac," Dillion replied.

The professor, a Middle Eastern man with a thick accent, entered and handed out syllabi.

"This course is intensive and meticulous," he said. "My office hours are listed on page three."

Dillion read carefully. Issac folded the syllabus and dozed off.

"Dude, do you just not care?" Dillion whispered.

"I got this. Relax. It's only the first day—fluff. I only came because attendance counts."

Dillion stared. How had someone so casual gotten into Georgetown? Maybe Issac was a secret genius.

“Okay, class, this is your assignment,” the professor announced.

He scribbled chapters and equations on the board. The first test was in two weeks.

After class, they exited the lecture hall.

“What class next?” Dillion asked.

“I’ve got downtime. Probably hit the café.”

“My next class is in an hour. I’ve got to go get a book.”

“People still go to the library? Bro, we have Google and Amazon.”

“I’m old school. I need hardcover books.”

“Work smarter, not harder. That’s college. Find the path of least resistance.”

“I like the path carved in stone, not painted on gravel.”

“You got it, bro. Later.”

Dillion walked across campus to the library, chasing a memory, a book his father once loved but he’d never bothered to read.

The library was quiet, almost like a museum. Dillion wandered the aisles, feeling like a relic in a sea of students raised on digital screens. As he scanned the shelves, a familiar voice chimed behind him.

“Are you stalking me?” Rebecca asked.

"I'm starting to think the same. What are you doing here? Your cousin doesn't believe in libraries."

"Isaac is special," she said, smiling. "He thinks charm, money, or family influence will get him through. It's worked so far."

"That a family philosophy?"

"For part of the family. Our dads are brothers. But my mom's different. She wasn't raised with money."

"I'm interested. What's your story?"

"Come to my table. I'll show you."

He helped her carry books to her table.

"I'm doing a project for independent studies: 'The Hidden History of D.C.' Did you know the street you ran down this morning? One street over—Volta Place—used to be a slave burial ground. Million-dollar homes stand on it now."

"Here in Georgetown?"

"Yep. Georgetown was a port town. The Potomac used to be dirty, overcrowded with ships. Tobacco from Potomac, Maryland, was dried here and shipped out."

"I just thought it was shops and the university."

"The university came first, then the neighborhood. Every city's got secrets. My major isn't history. It's international relations. My dad wants me to help take the family global," replied Rebecca.

"What does your family do?" asked Dillion.

“My dad and Isaac’s dad are hedge fund managers. They manage other people’s fortunes.”

“What about your mom’s side?”

“Scholars. My great-grandfather was a professor here. My mom’s a dean at American University.”

“That’s impressive.”

“Prestigious, yes. Lucrative, no.”

“My dad was a cop. My mom, a photographer.”

“We all have our role. I wanted to teach history like my mom, but my dad had other plans.”

“And you didn’t fight it?” Dillion asked.

Rebecca looked at him thoughtfully.

“I didn’t. But maybe I should have.”

Friday came all too quickly. The time was 4:30 a.m., and it was time for morning conditioning. Dillion had gone to bed in his workout clothes, ready for the grind. When the soft vibration of his phone buzzed under his pillow, he turned it off without hesitation. Three missed texts from Malia. He hadn’t called her in days—barely texted anything meaningful. School, lacrosse, and Rebecca were starting to consume him. He washed his face and brushed his teeth. It was time to train.

As he walked past Cooper Field, he glanced through the fence at the turf. Soon, he believed, fans be yelling his name here, just like they did back at high school. He saw the game in his head—scooping ground balls, dodging defenders, delivering crisp passes to his attackmen. He could score, sure, but setting others up? That was the art. Creating opportunities. That was his joy.

Today's strength training was at the John Thompson Jr. Intercollegiate Athletic Center. He'd only seen it from the outside—massive glass walls revealing rows of daunting machines. Football had priority here, but now it was lacrosse's turn.

The weight room was expansive, filled with every piece of equipment imaginable. Some teammates lingered, earbuds in, others stretched on the floor, preparing mentally for whatever Coach Yarling had in store. Dillion eagerly found a spot to sit and took it all in.

He remembered the first gym he ever entered: Spartan Gym. He was only eight. His father had found him a personal trainer, Coach Nik—a young, spry former football player with a passion for teaching. Nik didn't just teach Dillion how to work out; he taught him *why*. Discipline. Consistency. Principles. His father was sold.

At Spartan, Dillion had been intimidated. Older kids zoomed past him, strong and confident. But over time, he learned his body and grew stronger. Now, he was facing a new Spartan. A goliath. And this time, his father wasn't on the bench, watching with pride. This time, he had to look inward for strength.

Coach Yarling entered, followed by Head Coach Winn, who looked like a typical overly intense soccer dad; but when he spoke, the room stilled.

"Alright, guys. I know you've just started training. I've heard good things from Coach Yarling," he said, as the team formed a half-circle. "Just keep grinding. We've got strong returners this year. We'll be practicing soon and doing a Fall Ball game. For you younger guys, that's your chance to show me what you're ready for—but it starts *here*, in the weight room."

He paced as he spoke. "We'll have position meetings next week. Practice will be light, gloves and helmets only. No injuries before we even start. Equipment has sticks and cleats. Go see them after lifts, start stringing. I know some of you are religious about your stringing—go nuts."

Coach Winn gave a nod. "My door's always open in McDonough. If I'm not around, the assistants will know where to find me."

He stepped back. "Alright, good stretch today. We're seeing maxes. Some of you prima donnas couldn't lift a toothpick with a slice of cheese on it. But by season's start, I want Avengers. Let's get after it."

Lathan and Tim started stretches as several men entered—former players now coaches, each introduced by title and position. The one Dillion watched most closely was Coach Brian Phillips, offensive coordinator.

"Listen up," Coach Phillips called out, his voice slicing through the noise. "This year, we're running fast-paced offense—nonstop subs, fast breaks. Think Golden State meets lacrosse. The two-minute offense. Speed kills."

Dillion's heart raced. *That* was his style. He'd spent years in slow, methodical systems, waiting for the perfect strike. But this? This was *his* kind of ball—athleticism, creativity, chaos.

"Let's break up!" Coach Yarling shouted. Half the team moved to bench presses, the other to squat racks. Dillion started on squats, his least favorite. He preferred dumbbells, but Coach had other plans.

"Form, gentlemen," Yarling said. "Bad form gets you hurt. Good form gives you explosion. You want speed? Build the glutes."

He pointed at Dillion. "See this guy? Big butt, small calves—that's speed right there. Most of y'all need more glutes and less gut."

Dillion stood tall as the coach loaded 45-pound plates onto the bar.

"Feet shoulder-width apart. Squat like you're sitting on a stool, then explode up."

Dillion followed instructions. Smooth. Controlled.

"Good," Coach said, grabbing more weight. Dillion winced. He'd been at his limit, but he couldn't back down now. He had something to prove. Sweat beaded in his hair as he racked the bar and prepared for another set.

"Watch this form, gentlemen. This is power in the flesh." The assistants scribbled notes.

"Good job ... Frank ... Dillion ... whatever your name is," Coach said, waving him over. "Go do the vertical jump with Coach over there. Curious what your vertical is."

At the wall, Dillion stepped and leapt.

"Forty inches," the assistant called.

"Again."

Dillion felt tightness in his back from squats but jumped once more.

"Forty-two!"

"You could probably dunk a basketball. Good stuff. Sit-and-reach is next."

Around him, the gym buzzed. Everyone wanted to impress. Some looked like they regretted their off seasons.

After that, it all blurred. Dillion was in his element. He'd been training since he was four, when his father first put him in flag football. His dad once thought Dillion would follow in his footsteps. But football demanded quick reactions, not deep thought. And Dillion always *thought*. Too much.

He remembered one game: his father asked why he let a runner pass when he was in perfect position.

"My mouthpiece wasn't in," Dillion had replied. "I didn't want a penalty."

His father had laughed. "You think too much. Stick to lacrosse."

And now here he was.

As the session wound down, his body sore and his shirt soaked through, Dillion thought of the evening. He was going out with Rebecca. His chest tightened. That familiar excitement mixed with dread, like Christmas morning before unwrapping something fragile.

Coach Yarling approached. "Great job, Dillion. Those numbers today, remarkable for a freshman. Keep it up. I'm expecting big things."

Dillion had nothing left. He'd given everything.

Later, Yarling walked into Coach Winn's office.

"Hey, Winny?"

"You guys finish already?"

"Yeah. You've got something special with this group. Especially that kid—Frank."

"Dillion?"

"Yeah. If he plays like he lifts, he could be one of the most elite athletes I've seen. Especially for a freshman."

Coach Winn leaned back. "That's why we recruited him so hard. He lost his dad this summer. We backed off for a while, thought he wouldn't come. Made some transfer plays. Then he changed his mind. He's got a dogfight ahead for his spot, but the real battle?" He tapped his temple. "That's in his mind. And that one? That's the toughest fight."

"Well," Yarling said, "he's blue collar. Lunch-pail type. He's got a chip on his shoulder. He wants it."

"He'll get his chance," Coach Winn said. "One way or another."

Coach Yarling left the office and headed back down to the weight room to review the performance results. He began drafting individualized workout regimens for each athlete, aiming to increase their max lifts by the start of the season. Still, he couldn't shake how impressed he was with Dillion's workout. The freshman had earned his respect.

Chapter 11: Man Up

In lacrosse, a "man-up" situation tests your edge—when the other team is a man down, and it's your job to capitalize. No excuses. No hesitation. Dillion's life had entered its own man-up moment. With no father to guide him, no one to fall back on, and expectations mounting, it was time to execute. Alone, but not unprepared. The field was different now, but the mission was the same: rise or fade.

Dillion spent the rest of the day in class, his thoughts drifting often to the evening ahead. He was excited—nervous, even. He and Isaac had gone to the store the day before to get the outfit Rebecca had described through Isaac. Of course, Isaac added his own flair to the look—something a little bolder, a little more stylish.

But as Dillion ran through imagined scenarios of the evening in his mind, another face kept surfacing: Malia's. A slow unease crept in. Was he starting to neglect her? He'd already been emotionally distant from his mother; was he doing the same to the person who had always been there for him? Malia had been part of his life longer than most. They always supported each other.

His thumb hovered over her contact. Anxiety pulsed through his veins at the thought of calling. Still, he knew he had to. He pressed the button.

"Hello?"

"Hey…"

"What's up, stranger?"

"Nothing, just returning your calls. Sorry I've been wrapped up with class and everything."

"I think we both have," she said, her voice softening. "But it's okay. You know I always find time to bother you. What are you up to?"

“Nothing much. I’m heading to a charity event.”

“A charity event? Like what?” Malia was surprised.

“A symphony. It’s for a good cause.”

“You? At a symphony?”

“Yeah,” Dillion chuckled. “Like I said, it’s for charity.”

“This a lacrosse thing? I’m confused.”

“No, just ... doing different things with different people. Broadening my horizons, right? That’s what college is for.”

“I guess ... if that’s how you feel. Well, have fun at least.”

“I will. I’ll call you later.”

“Okay. Just text me if it gets too late.”

“Will do.”

Dillion ended the call with a quiet sense of peace. He had talked to Malia. He had done what his heart demanded. For now, it was enough. Now it was time to meet Rebecca.

He walked to the front of the school past the resting statue of John Carroll, the school’s founder. At precisely 7 o'clock, as directed, he spotted Rebecca already waiting for him at 3700 O St. She was seated in an Uber, the vehicle a midsized Nissan. She dressed impeccably, appearing radiant in the soft glow of the evening.

“You’re punctual. I like that,” Rebecca said, sliding over to make room for him.

The car had that unmistakable new-car smell, spotless inside. The driver never looked back, his eyes locked on the road like he was chauffeuring a diplomat.

“So, are you excited?” Rebecca asked, glancing sideways at Dillion.

“Umm … I wouldn’t say excited. More curious, I guess,” Dillion replied, turning to look out the window, trying to avoid eye contact.

“It’ll be fun. My father will be there. You’ll get to meet him.”

“Your *father*?”

“Yeah. He’s a major contributor to the charity and pretty involved in alumni affairs. You’re meeting some heavy hitters tonight, small fry,” she said with a grin. “He’s a big lacrosse guy too. He can talk forever—just a heads-up.”

“I can do lacrosse. The rest of it ... not so much.”

“Just stick close to me. I’ll show you the ropes.”

As the Uber neared the venue, Rebecca pulled a small prescription bottle from her clutch and discreetly took out two pills.

“What’s that?” Dillion asked, watching her swallow them.

“One’s for the soreness from my injury, and the other helps me focus. I get distracted sometimes.”

“Anxiety? You?” He looked surprised. “You’re such a social butterfly.”

“I know, right?” She gave a half-smile. “I love being around people, but sometimes it gets overwhelming. I start thinking everyone’s judging me ... whether I'm pretty enough, smiling enough. The meds help me stay calm. Keep the stress at bay."

The car came to an abrupt stop.

"We're here," she said.

They stepped out into a long line of cars that were unloading guests. All around them was a sea of black and white formal wear, people moving in clusters, their voices low and polished.

"This is going to be *great*," Rebecca said, eagerly scanning the crowd for a familiar face.

Dillion adjusted the bow tie Isaac had insisted he wear. His hard-soled shoes clicked against the pavement as he followed her through the crowd. He had no idea where they were going or who she was looking for. He was out of his element—completely at her mercy. This was her world, not his. All he could do was embrace the unfamiliar.

"So, who are we meeting?" Dillion asked as Rebecca led him deeper into the crowd.

"My dad," she said, checking her phone. "He just texted. He's waiting up front."

As they approached the front of the Kennedy Center, the crowd began to thicken. Rebecca reached for Dillion's hand. He froze.

The moment her hand touched his, a surge of awkward electricity shot through him. His mind raced: *Should I hold it back? Grip firmly? Be subtle?* He glanced at her, hoping for a signal, but her eyes were fixed ahead, feet rising on tiptoes as she scanned the crowd. She seemed unaware of what she'd done, impulse or intention, he couldn't tell. Still, Dillion held her hand firmly.

"Rebecca, over here!" called a sovereign voice from the crowd.

It was her father—a slim, impeccably groomed man with hair like cotton balls and a sharp, stiletto-pointed nose that mirrored Rebecca's, though it suited her more gracefully. Beside him stood her mother, a petite woman with deep black hair and thick-rimmed glasses that had, with time, become fashionable rather than outdated. Together they made sense—extravagance paired with simplicity. Dillion thought: *Of course. That's how Rebecca came to be.*

"Daddy!" Rebecca exclaimed, darting toward him and forgetting Dillion's hand. He stood adrift in the crowd, unsure whether to follow or wait.

"Dillion! Over here!" she called, turning back.

He hesitated. *Was he supposed to be meeting her family like this?* He hadn't prepared for a full meet-and-greet. What was her last name again—Loudain?

"You must be Dillion," her father said, stepping forward. "We've heard quite a bit about you. Isaac's roommate, right?"

"Yes, sir. Nice to meet you," Dillion said, offering a handshake.

"Isaac says you're quite the lacrosse player. It's about time we brought in some fresh talent. I'm always pushing for another championship. Yale just snagged one, and I think it's our year."

"I agree, sir. We've got a strong squad."

"Well said." He turned. "This is my wife, Wanda."

"Hello, Dillion," she said warmly. "You're in for a treat tonight. Chopin is my favorite."

"This will be my first symphony, ma'am. I'm looking forward to it."

Rebecca returned and slipped her hand into Dillion's once again. "Hope we're not bombarding you with questions."

"No, not at all," he said, unsure of anything but her warmth.

"Let's find our seats," she said.

The grandeur of the Kennedy Center unfolded as they entered the mezzanine. Every detail—the gleam of chandeliers, the velvet of the carpet, the sweeping architecture—radiated elegance. The orchestra was settling in. Dillion grabbed a playbill, hoping to commemorate the moment.

Rebecca floated through the aisle, greeting familiar faces, exchanging cheek kisses. Dillion sat alone, absorbing the atmosphere. The tuning of violins sliced the murmuring air. Then the lights dimmed, and applause filled the hall as the maestro and soloist took their places.

Rebecca returned and placed her hand gently over his. Dillion tensed. *Was this still friendliness? Or something else now?*

The maestro raised his arms, graceful and fluid, like a willow in wind light. The first notes of the nocturne floated out like spun silk.

Rebecca leaned in, her head resting on the curve of Dillion's neck.

"This is my favorite, Nocturne No. 9," she whispered.

The music surged. And then … memory struck.

It was the same piece his father had been playing that night. *Prom. The car ride. The crash. The hospital. Malia. Mom. Dad.*

The music, now too familiar, too sharp, dragged the memory forward. His eyes stung. Tears threatened.

Rebecca, unaware of his spiraling thoughts, whispered again. "It's Chopin's Piano Concerto No. 2. You know why they play classical music in elevators? It's to help you ascend and descend—emotionally. That's how this feels to me. Like my spirit's going somewhere. The music detoxes you. Makes space for something new."

Dillion stared ahead, her voice echoing through him like another instrument. *Did she know what she was saying? Did she realize how perfectly her words matched what he was feeling?*

"This is one of the few pieces Chopin composed with an orchestra," she continued, her voice low and reverent. "Most of his works are for solo piano. But life isn't solo, right? It's about blending—different instruments, different people—creating something more."

Dillion was silent. The grief, the beauty, the surreal pull of it all; it overwhelmed him. And yet, he didn't want to leave it. For the first time in weeks, he wasn't running from his emotions. He was *in* them. Living them. The music invited him to.

The fragrance of Rebecca's perfume, soft and floral, anchored him in the moment. He wondered if he could get used to that scent every day.

When the final note echoed into stillness, the hall erupted in applause. Dillion rose to his feet, clapping without restraint.

"Wow," Rebecca said, her eyes wide. "Wasn't that incredible?"

"Amazing," Dillion replied. "I don't know what could top it."

"I've got an idea. Sushi?" she said as they approached the entrance.

“I’m more of a taco guy, but when in Rome…”

“There’s this perfect little spot on the waterfront—Mate. Best crab salad and martinis.”

“I don’t drink, but I’ll judge that crab salad. Maryland guys *know* crab,” he grinned.

At the curb, she waved at the arriving Uber. Dillion reached for her hand, this time without hesitation. She looked at him, surprised. Then smiled—warm, inviting.

“Where are your parents?” he asked.

“Socializing. My dad lives for this. See where I get it from?” she said as she opened the car door. “But I’m starving.”

The ride was short—just across Rock Creek to 31st and K Street. Mate was tucked into the corner like a secret. Through its glass front, Dillion saw soft lights, abstract art, and silhouettes of diners in quiet conversation.

“This is it!” Rebecca said, gleaming. “Isn’t it perfect?”

Dillion stepped out and held the door for her. The scent of sesame oil and seared tuna drifted past as they entered. A hostess greeted them. At Rebecca’s request, they were seated beside the sushi bar.

Rebecca slid off her coat, her eyes scanning the menu with glee.

“The volcano rolls are to die for.”

Dillion stared at the unfamiliar names and images.

“So …” he asked, looking up at her, “what should I order? This is your world.”

“Hmm ... you just can’t go wrong with the volcano roll,” Rebecca said, flipping the menu closed with certainty.

“Alright, I’ll get that too,” Dillion replied as he stretched his legs along the bottom rail of the tall barstool.

The waiter arrived. Rebecca took the lead.

“We’ll have two volcano rolls, and I’ll have an extra dry martini with grenadine.”

“Will that be all?” the waiter asked, turning to Dillion.

“She’s the boss. Maybe just a Sprite,” Dillion said as he handed over his menu.

They settled into a comfortable silence while waiting for their food. Rebecca sipped her martini slowly, with poise.

“So ... why did you invite me to this charity event?” Dillion asked, brushing condensation off his glass. He tried to sound casual, though the question weighed on him.

“Because I have a crush on you,” Rebecca answered simply, taking another sip of her drink.

“Really? Who just says that?” Dillion blinked, stunned. That was not how he expected the night to begin. Before he could say more, the waiter returned and placed the sushi in front of them.

“Oh my god, these look so good,” Rebecca said, reaching for her clutch. “I’ll be right back—I need the powder room.”

Dillion looked down at his plate. The rolls were neatly arranged, with a small serving of crab salad. There were chopsticks in a paper wrapper ... and a fork. He chose the fork, broke the top of the roll, and carefully scooped a bite into his mouth.

Rebecca returned and paused as she glanced at his plate.

"Umm ... you can't do that," she said.

"Do what?" Dillion asked, as he took another bite.

"Use a fork for sushi."

"What do you mean? It's not like I'm eating it with a spoon."

"You're supposed to use chopsticks."

"I don't know how. I thought they were for rice or noodle dishes."

"No, they're for sushi too. Here, let me show you."

She slid the sticks out of their wrapper, arranged them effortlessly between her fingers, and picked up a roll in one clean motion.

"See? Easy."

Dillion followed her lead. He tried to mimic her grip, but the chopsticks slipped from his fingers and landed with a soft clatter on the table.

"I'll just stick to the fork for now."

"I will leave right now if you keep eating that sushi with a fork."

"It's that serious?"

"Yes. It's like ... eating fried chicken and leaving meat on the bone."

"How do you even know I like fried chicken?"

"Everyone loves fried chicken, Dillion."

"What do fried chicken and sushi even have to do with each other?"

"Nothing. It's about respect. You don't leave food behind. You eat it right."

He laughed. "That's funny. My mom used to leave meat on the bone, and my dad would always take her plate and eat what was left."

She smiled. "So, use the chopsticks. It's a rite of passage."

"It's just awkward."

"Everything's awkward at first. Wasn't lacrosse awkward when you started?"

"I honestly can't remember when I started. It's been part of my life so long ... but yeah, you have a point."

"So how did you start playing?"

"As far back as I can remember, I've had a stick in my hand. I played a bunch of sports, but lacrosse just clicked."

"Did your dad play?"

"No. He actually didn't know anything about it. But he wanted me to try something different, something outside the usual path. He believed in pushing past comfort zones."

Rebecca leaned in, listening closely.

"He used to sign me up for elite camps, and then he'd go back and teach everything he learned to kids who couldn't afford that kind of training. He'd make sure I played on teams that weren't the best, but the most diverse. He wanted other kids to see that we didn't have to follow the same script."

"That's really admirable. How did you feel about it?"

"At first, I didn't think much of it. I just knew I was playing with kids who weren't at my level, and it frustrated me sometimes. But my dad made it an adventure. He wanted to prove that kids—especially Black kids—could be great at something different. Lacrosse became his mission."

"So, it was his passion."

"Exactly. I don't even know if it was mine. It became our shared dream."

Rebecca hesitated for a moment, then asked, "So what is your passion, Dillion?"

"You," he said, grinning as he awkwardly picked up the chopsticks again and fumbled a roll into his mouth.

Rebecca burst into laughter, loud enough to make a few heads turn.

"That was smooth," she said, reaching for her martini.

Dillion leaned back.

"Here's a question for you … since you're mixed, who do you identify with?" asked Rebecca.

"Well, I was raised in a diverse community. It wasn't really a big issue. My dad always told me to just be myself. Know the history, understand where we come from, but don't let it box you in."

"Did I offend you?"

"No. I think the better question is: what do I identify with? And that's someone who's just trying to be happy. I want to find my purpose and live honestly. That's why I'm here at Georgetown—to explore."

"Why Georgetown?"

Dillion's voice dropped slightly. "It was my dad's last big dream for me before he passed."

Rebecca froze, her expression softening. "I'm sorry. Was that too soon to bring up?"

Dillion shook his head.

"Honestly? Was this the right time?"

"No, it's fine," Dillion said. "He wanted this for me for a reason. I guess he hoped I'd meet people like Rebeccas and Issacs, to see there's a different way to live. Is it for me? I guess I'll find out."

"How are you liking campus so far?" Rebecca asked.

"It's fun. No complaints. I'm just figuring it out as I go."

"How's your mom handling it?"

"She supports whatever I do. I haven't really talked to her much since I got here. I'm just ... not ready to live in the past. She's still dealing with my father's death, and I just want to move forward."

Rebecca's voice softened. "Don't you think she needs you? Even just a little?"

"Yeah ... she probably does. But I can't live in the past and expect to build a future. I'm doing this for all of us—for her, for Dad, and for me."

"That's really deep. Are you sure you're just a freshman?"

Dillion smiled. "It's how I was raised. Fight through adversity, no matter what form it takes. This is just another version of that. It hurts. The memories are still fresh. But I've got to keep my focus on the future and my goals."

"What are those goals?"

"Become the face of Georgetown Lacrosse. And win a national championship—this year."

Rebecca raised her eyebrows. "Whew, cowboy. This year? You've got some stiff competition, and you guys didn't even crack the top ten in the preseason polls."

"I'll show you better than I can tell you."

Rebecca glanced down at his plate. "Well, you're definitely becoming a pro with the chopsticks."

Dillion followed her gaze. His plate was clean. Even the scraps of crab salad had vanished, expertly picked up with the tips of his sticks.

"Let's go," Rebecca said, setting her credit card on the table. "Dinner's on me tonight, only because I convinced you to come to Georgetown. Next time's on you."

“Next time? There’s a next time?”

“Well, there’s still time for you to mess it up between here and my house. But yeah, next time.”

“Okay, I can do that. But I wouldn’t even know where to take you. This is your town.”

“We’ll figure it out. Button your jacket, it’s chilly tonight. We’re walking. It’s not far, and the stars are out. Just remember what I said about messing it up.”

Dillion glanced at her with concern. “You sure your leg’s okay for the walk?”

“That’s what these are for,” she said, pulling a pill bottle from her clutch, popping a tablet, and washing it down with the last of her martini.

“C’mon,” she said, slipping her card back into her clutch and taking Dillion’s hand.

They stepped outside into the cool night air. Rebecca gestured down the sidewalk.

“This is Wisconsin Avenue. It starts here and stretches all the way into Maryland. It’s one of the biggest thoroughfares in the city. We’ll walk up a bit, make a left on O Street. That’ll take us to my place, and then to campus.”

“I think I remember that from our morning runs,” Dillion said.

“Yup. You run right along M Street. You’re learning,” she said, smiling up at him.

“This is nice,” Dillion said, his voice sincere. “Thank you for inviting me tonight.”

“You’re pretty cool,” Rebecca said. “I knew it’d be fun, but you’re something else—a breath of fresh air. You’re exactly what we need around here.”

Chapter 12: Restraining Box

In lacrosse, the restraining box holds you back—literally. You stay inside it until the moment's right to break free, to charge into play, to make your move. For Dillion, the box wasn't chalk lines. It was guilt, pressure, and choices. Rebecca stirred something new. Malia reminded him of who he was. And his own ambition? That was the clock ticking, daring him to break out before it was too late.

"So, this is it. You want to come in?" Rebecca asked softly.

Dillion shook his head. "Not tonight. It's pretty late, and I've got training in the morning."

"You guys train on Saturdays now?"

"No, but *I* do. I told you: we're winning the championship this year. I've got to train when everyone else is relaxing. While you're eating your Honey Nut Cheerios, I'll be training. While they're nursing hangovers, I'll be grinding." He chuckled, half-joking, half-dead serious.

Rebecca gave him a half-amused, half-admiring look. "I guess that's good ... but one of these weekends, you're gonna have to let your hair down, especially before the season starts."

"The season already started. It started when I signed my acceptance letter. This is for my dad; for the legacy he wanted us to build."

She studied him for a beat. "But what about your own legacy, your own quest, Dillion?"

"There's time for that. First things first," he said, leaning in to kiss her on the cheek.

Rebecca lingered in the doorway, glancing back to see if he'd changed his mind. But he didn't. His posture was calm, steady, unmoving. She felt the strength of his will.

"Good night, Dillion."

"I'll text you when I get settled. Good night."

He turned and walked away, the cold air brushing his skin as the distant sound of Chopin and Mozart floated through his mind. He felt ... different. Elevated. Like something was transforming inside him. A tingling sensation pulsed through his chest.

Just as the night replayed itself in his thoughts, his phone rang.

Rebecca? It was too soon.

"Hello?"

"Hey, I was worried about you," Malia's voice said gently. "I know you were going out tonight, but I had this knot in my stomach, so I decided to call."

"I'm good. I'm actually just getting back to my dorm."

"Oh, that's a relief. Maybe it was the hummus I had earlier." She laughed lightly. "Now I can sleep."

"Yeah, I'm fine, Malia."

"How was your night?"

"It was great. Good to get off campus for a bit. What about you?"

"Just a sorority meet-and-greet thingy. So ... who'd you go out with?"

"A friend of a friend."

"Does this *friend of a friend* have a name?"

"Rebecca."

"Oh, so it's a girl. *Friend.*"

"Yeah. She's my roommate's cousin. She's just ... nice. That's all."

"I didn't say anything. I'm not your mom, Dillion, I'm your friend. You can tell me stuff."

"It's just weird, that's all. Like, hey Malia, I'm going on a date!" he said, sarcastically.

"I get it. Just don't beat around the bush next time."

"So ... it's your roommate's cousin, huh?"

"Yeah. She's a friend."

"You've already made that clear," she said, quieter now.

"Have fun. That's what we went to college for: meeting new people, enjoying life, right? Just ... be careful. I really did have a knot in my stomach tonight."

"I will. Promise. And it's not like that, Malia."

"Yeah ... just not *yet*. Don't be so defensive. You always get that way when you're nervous. I know you, Dillion."

"Good night, Malia."

"Good night. It'd be nice to see *your* name on my caller ID for once. Feels like you're trying to edge me out. I can only fight for so long."

Dillion woke at 4:30 a.m. sharp. He threw on his Georgetown hoodie, shorts, and Brooks running shoes. Long-distance today. Time to push harder than ever.

He hit the pavement and stretched beneath the early morning sky. His first obstacle: the Exorcist Steps. Brutal. He sprinted them, conditioning each muscle to remember the burn, the climb. Then came the Key Bridge. Then the long stretch of M Street.

He timed his pace. Six-minute mile next week. No excuses. No mediocrity.

But the thoughts came, uninvited. The memory of last night. The rush. The new town. The new him. And then—guilt.

When was the last time I called Mom? Am I turning my back on her?

Am I forgetting who I am?

Am I pushing Malia away, too?

With each stride, the thoughts grew louder. Was he running to build himself, or running from what he was afraid to face? He didn't want to think about it. He felt strong in his stance, unmoved. But deep inside, the feeling of loss sat heavy. Like the day he lost the championship game. Except now, instead of sulking, he knew he had to face it. He needed to go home.

After the run, Dillion stepped into the shower. The hot water pounded his sore muscles. The lavender-scented soap filled the air, calming him. As he dried off with the plush towel, he glanced at his phone.

Call Mom.

Before he could, it buzzed.

Malia.

“Hey, you must be a mind reader,” Dillion said, placing the phone on speaker as he dried his hair.

“What do you mean?” she asked.

“I was just thinking of going home today. You were on my mind.”

“That’s crazy! My mom’s on her way to pick me up right now. How were you planning to get home?”

“I was gonna take the train into Aberdeen and figure the rest out. I thought it’d be nice to surprise Mom ... and hoped you’d be there too. Looks like it’s all working out.”

“Yeah, since I can’t have a car on campus, Mom offered to grab me for the weekend. I was getting a little homesick, and I forgot a bunch of stuff when I packed.”

“Well then ... I guess I’ll see you soon.”

“Wait! We can pick you up from the train station on the way if you want. I’ll just call Mom and let her know the new plan!”

“Just make sure your mom doesn’t call mine. I want it to be a surprise.”

“Okay—will do. Or rather, *won’t* do. Just call me when you get to the station.”

“Cool.”

Dillion threw on a pair of jeans, his Georgetown hoodie, and his running shoes faster than usual. He didn't normally like to rush, but something about this morning felt good—urgent in a way that mattered.

His ride share arrived; he was headed toward Union Station. He hoped the next train would line up perfectly with his arrival, and when he stepped into the terminal, the glowing departure board rewarded him—ten minutes until departure. Perfect.

On the platform, a breeze funneled through the tunnel and cooled his forehead. The train's headlights flickered through the haze, and as it pulled in, he stepped aboard and found a window seat. The hum of the train, the rhythm of movement brought back memories. Day trips with his dad. Museum visits. Street maps and life lessons. His father had always insisted that being street smart was just as important as being book smart. Dillion was grateful now. It all felt like preparation.

Chapter 13: The Penalty Box

In lacrosse, the penalty box is where you sit after a foul—watching, waiting, stewing in the consequences. No stick in your hand. No way to change the play. Just time ticking down, and a pit in your stomach. For Dillion, stepping into his childhood home felt like walking straight into that box. The rules had changed, and no one told him. His mother had crossed a line, and suddenly, he wasn't sure whose game this was anymore or whether he even wanted to keep playing.

The train pulled away, transforming scenery from D.C.'s dense cityscape to the sparser, open edges that stretched toward Baltimore and beyond. Then rural views emerged like a memory—wide fields and modest homes. It was closer to home. The nostalgia was sharp, but so was something else: a quiet thrill. He felt like he was doing something bold by coming back by confronting a part of himself he hadn't looked at in a while.

His phone buzzed before he could call Malia.

"You're on a roll today," Dillion said, placing it to his cheek.

"I don't know if you're close yet, but we made good time. We're in the parking lot waiting."

"Perfect. I'm about eight, maybe nine minutes out."

"Cool. We're in the wagon," she chuckled.

Dillion smiled. As he hung up, the train began to slow. He'd arrived.

Stepping off, the shift hit him hard—the rush of the city replaced by open skies, smaller streets, and familiar silence. He spotted her instantly—bright red bomber jacket, arms waving as if he couldn't possibly miss her in the nearly empty lot.

"Hey, stranger!" Malia called out, beaming.

Dillion grinned as she practically leapt into his arms. Her hug hit him like a tackle.

"Whoa there," he laughed. "You must've really missed me."

"Duh, silly," she mumbled into his chest.

Layla, Malia's mom, stepped up for a hug after Malia finally let go.

"Good to have you back, Dillion," she said warmly, eyeing his hair with familiar judgment. "Don't they have barbers in Georgetown?"

"I'm going for a new look; it's in the 'growing' phase," he said, lightly tugging his ends.

"Mmm. I suppose." She was still in her hospital scrubs. Classic Layla, always on the move.

They climbed into the car. Dillion took his old spot in the back seat as gospel music played softly on the radio. It all felt eerily the same.

"So, Dillion," Layla began as she merged into traffic. "How's school going?"

"It's good. Classes are solid. Lacrosse is heating up."

"Dillion has a *girlfriend*, Mom," Malia teased with a smirk.

"A girlfriend, Dillion?" Layla turned around briefly, forgetting she was still driving.

"No! I'm just meeting people, making friends. Malia's just jealous."

"Really?" Malia quipped, rolling her eyes.

Dillion tried changing the subject. “So, how’s everything around here? You been spending time with my mom?”

“Here and there,” Layla replied. “Work’s been hectic. Flu season prep. I haven’t even watched my court shows. That tells you how crazy it’s been.”

“No court shows? You really must be busy,” Dillion said, watching the scenery roll by.

Soon, they turned into the neighborhood. The court felt oddly surreal, like walking into a paused dream. Though he hadn’t been gone long, it felt like years.

“You coming over first, or going straight home?” Malia asked. “I was hoping you could grab a box from the attic while you're here.”

“I’ll come over for a second. No big deal,” Dillion replied, adjusting his backpack.

As they stepped inside, the familiar smell hit him. He glanced around half-expecting a new picture or couch throw, but everything was exactly the same. Then, his eyes landed on something: an old, dusty cage behind the couch.

“What ever happened to Bunny?” he asked.

“After all these years, you ask about Bunny?”

“It just crossed my mind. I guess life got busy. I forgot.”

“Well ... after Grandma passed, I let Bunny go.”

“What? I didn’t know that.”

“I thought Bunny should be free. I wasn’t in a place to care for him the way he deserved. None of us were.”

“But you kept the cage?”

“Yeah,” Malia said softly. “I never had the heart to toss it.”

“You think he’ll come back?”

“No. But he’s part of me. Last week, I got a bunny face tattoo on my ankle.”

“You *what*? You got a tattoo? I think the world’s ending.”

She pulled up her pant leg to reveal a small white rabbit face just above her ankle.

“That’s ... actually cute.” Dillion chuckled, surprised.

He found himself wondering why she never told him. Malia *always* told him everything. Maybe she’d needed space. Maybe letting Bunny go was her way of making peace.

“Okay, I’m gonna head home,” Dillion said, grabbing the attic boxes.

“Want me to walk with you?”

“You can if you want.”

“Okay. But I have to tell you, Mom hasn’t really been herself lately. She kind of pushed my mom away. So go over with an open mind.”

“Open mind?”

"Yeah," Malia said, eyes dropping to the hardwood floor as if she'd just lost something important.

Dillion and Malia stepped outside and walked toward the house where Dillion was raised. It looked the same: the aging shutters, the worn siding, and the garden—overgrown but still hanging on. He figured the fading upkeep was just the changing season. But something felt off.

Then he saw the car.

Parked beside his old Pontiac was a vehicle he knew. Too familiar.

"Whose car is that?" Dillion asked, turning to Malia. "It looks familiar."

Malia didn't answer.

Dillion approached the door and gently pushed it open. His mother always left it unlocked. She was old-school, a country woman who still believed in the good of people.

Inside, boxes lined the walls. In the kitchen, sleek new appliances gleamed. Pressure cookers sat in a row against the backsplash, unopened and unused.

"What is all this?" Dillion muttered, scanning the room like a stranger.

"Mom!" he called out as he moved toward the living room.

There was a faint sound. Laughter. A television?

"Mom?" he called again. His voice echoed back.

He noticed the basement door was cracked open, light spilling from below. Malia edged closer, as if they were walking into something they weren't supposed to see.

Dillion led the way, descending the steps slowly, careful not to make noise. The voices below became clearer. His mother's. And another voice—familiar. Too familiar.

When he reached the bottom, he stopped cold.

"Mom? Coach Simmons? What is going on?"

His mother was perched on Coach Simmons' lap, laughing as if this were normal.

"Dillion?" she gasped, jumping up like a kid caught sneaking a peek at their birthday presents.

"Question is, what are you doing?" Dillion said, heat rising in his face.

"We were just talking, that's all!" Tasha said, stepping toward him.

"I think you need to leave, Coach," Dillion said, stepping aside and motioning toward the door.

"He doesn't have to leave. This is my house," she said, folding her arms.

"Last I checked, Dad left this house to me. And I'm pretty sure Mrs. Simmons would prefer her husband home."

Coach Simmons said nothing. He grabbed his keys and left, silent and quick.

Malia lingered on the stairs, unsure whether to stay or follow.

"My father isn't even cold in the ground, and this is what's happening?"

"What? I'm just having an adult conversation."

"Is that what it's called now?"

"You haven't been calling. You haven't even tried talking to me."

"He gave everything for this house—for this family—and now you're here acting like it's no big deal?"

"This is my house! I kept it going. I took care of both of you. I'm allowed to live my life."

Dillion turned and stormed up the stairs. His mother followed. Malia waited a second, then followed too.

In the kitchen, Dillion tripped over a stack of boxes scattered near the island.

"And what are all these boxes?" he asked, trying to hide his stumble. "Why do you have all this junk? It looks like a hoarder's house."

He moved to the sink, inspecting the clutter of unopened gadgets.

"I need them. I have plans. I'm going to start entertaining again," Tasha said, clutching a box of silverware like it was something sacred.

"This is insane," Dillion muttered, brushing past rows of crockpots lined up like museum pieces.

"At least these things will never leave me. Everyone else has. Do you even care, Dillion? You're just like your father. Maybe worse. At least he pretended to care about me for your sake."

“What? He loved you. He loved all of us.”

Malia stood off to the side, silent.

“Malia, did you know about this?” Dillion turned suddenly, voice rising.

“I … I didn’t know,” she said, taken aback. She hadn’t expected him to turn on her.

“Someone knew something,” he snapped, spinning around, eyes darting from pile to pile of boxes, fists clenched like he might throw something. “It’s all too much.”

“I told you to call home,” Tasha said. “I texted; I begged you. You left. And now you show up like the world should’ve paused just for you? If you don’t tend your garden, weeds will grow.”

Malia stepped forward, something hardening in her voice.

“She’s right,” she said, quiet but firm. “You walked away, Dillion. On her. On me. She just didn’t say it because she’s your mother.”

Dillion looked stunned.

“So, you’re all just in on this? I haven’t even been gone a full semester, and already I’m being shut out, my father’s memory trampled. I guess the saying is true: time waits for no man.”

He snatched the Pontiac keys from the hook near the door and walked out, his backpack slung over one shoulder.

The Pontiac roared to life, and Dillion drove fast, too fast. His mind spiraled. He kept replaying the scene—his mother, Coach Simmons, the boxes, Malia’s silence. Had he been too distracted by school, lacrosse, Rebecca?

No. They owed him loyalty. If not to him, then to his father. The man who built that house. The man they all seemed to forget.

But did the living owe the dead anything? Did they owe *him* anything? Yes. In his mind, they did.

His phone buzzed in his lap. He grabbed it and called Rebecca. She answered after several rings.

“Hello?” Her voice was distracted, maybe annoyed.

“Hey. Is it okay if I swing by in about an hour?”

“Sure. I’m at a cocktail party, but we’re wrapping up. Is everything okay? Isaac said you went home.”

“Yeah. I just need to clear my head. If you’re busy, I can just go to the dorm.”

“No, it’s okay. Just call me when you’re close.”

“Okay.” He ended the call and put the phone beside him.

She would understand. If not her, then no one would.

The car smelled like it hadn’t been driven in months. A leak in the window let in the occasional whiff of musk. The old Pontiac hadn’t moved since prom. It was the last gift his father ever gave him.

He merged onto the parkway, cutting across toward Georgetown. Took the back route—Cabin John to Canal Road. Then he called.

"I'm here. I'll be there in 10."

"How did you get here so fast?"

"I drove."

"Umm, okay ... well, the door's open."

Dillion found a parking spot a block away from Rebecca's apartment. It was tight, but he'd mastered the art of parallel parking. As he shut the door, he glanced around. Would anyone try to break into the car? He'd seen shattered glass on the street before while running through this neighborhood, like breadcrumbs from some silent theft. He always wondered: did the thief get what they wanted? Was it worth the risk? Did they ever get caught?

He left his car unlocked. He had no choice; the lock was busted. But he didn't own anything of value. If someone rummaged through, they'd be disappointed.

Just as he looked up, a blinding light swung around the corner. The kind he'd only seen on TV. Police headlights. Maybe they were looking for the same people who shattered the glass he always saw on the street. Good, he thought. Let them catch them.

A small wave of ease washed over him. At least someone was trying to stop the chaos. He tightened his hoodie against the chill and started walking toward Rebecca's building.

"Hello, sir. Mind if we have a word with you?"

Dillion paused, confused. Maybe they thought he saw something?

"Sure," he said hesitantly. "But I just got out of the car."

Then came the voice from the cruiser radio:

"Suspect is approximately six-foot Black male, light-colored hoodie…"

Dillion's breath caught. He looked down at his white Georgetown hoodie. Surely they didn't mean *him*. He was a student. His father was a cop. But how would they know that?

"Sir, we need you to stop." The tone had shifted from polite to command.

Anxiety tightened in Dillion's chest. Not now. Not this.

He froze.

"Can you take your hands out of your pockets—for your safety and mine," one officer said, flashlight beam blinding Dillion.

"Yes, sir."

Cooperate. That's what his father always said. Be calm, respectful, and you'll be fine.

"What's in the backpack?" the officer asked.

Dillion had forgotten it was even on his shoulder. He slipped it off slowly.

"Just clothes. I'm a student at Georgetown."

"Do you have your student ID?"

He patted his pockets. Nothing.

Then it hit him: he left his wallet at Malia's house. In his rush, he hadn't gone back for it.

"You mind opening the bag for us?" another officer asked.

Dillion hesitated. He was losing his grip, emotionally and mentally. A third police car rolled up.

"Look, I'm a student. I play lacrosse at Georgetown. I just left my ID at a friend's place."

His father's words came back. *If you ever get stopped—don't say too much. Call me.* But he couldn't call. Not now.

"What's your name, buddy?" one officer, a Black man, asked.

"Am I being detained? Am I free to leave?"

The other, a Hispanic officer, answered, "You match the description of a suspect in a vehicle break-in nearby."

"So now what?" Dillion asked, backpack still in his hands.

"We're going to conduct a show-up. We have a witness. They'll tell us if you're the guy."

"My friend lives right up the street. She can vouch for me," he pleaded.

"Just stay where you are. This won't take long—it's just procedure."

From the corner of his eye, Dillion saw window blinds shift above him. People were watching; neighbors were peering down like spectators. Hidden but curious.

Could anyone really identify someone at night in a hoodie? Was there even a witness? Or was this just what happened?

"Can I make a phone call?"

"After we do what we need to do, you can call whoever you want."

His phone buzzed in his pocket. Rebecca. He dared to reach for it. The spotlight from the police car washed over him. He stood frozen, his silhouette thrown across the sidewalk.

He felt like a criminal. For the first time in his life, he understood why people ran. The pressure, the fear—it made sense now. But he didn't run. His father would never forgive him. And if he ran and they caught him, even innocence wouldn't protect him then.

"You look a little jumpy," one officer said. "Do we need to cuff you?"

Every instinct in his body screamed run, but he stayed still. The cuffs clicked cold around his wrists, heavy like guilt. The officers sat him on the sidewalk; legs crossed like a detainee.

Another car pulled up. The spotlight shifted, bright on his face. He turned to the left, then to the right. And waited. The radio crackled.

"That's a negative on the show-up."

The cuffs came off. His wrists burned from the pressure. He was free, but not really.

As they let him go, he felt violated. His skin crawled. Was this because he was Black? Or did he just *fit the description*? If that "witness" had said yes, what would've happened?

Was his fear exaggerated? Was it media-fed? Or had he just experienced what so many already knew to be true?

His phone vibrated again. *Rebecca.*

Chapter 14: Man Down

In lacrosse, "man down" means you're outnumbered. A player's mistake has left your team exposed, vulnerable. You dig in, hoping to survive the penalty time without breaking. But what if the one who's down is you? Off the field, Dillion felt like he was the one who'd committed the foul—misreading people, missing signals, pushing the wrong ones away. And now, in a room that wasn't his, with a girl who couldn't save him, he realized something: being man down wasn't just about losing ground. It was about fighting like hell to stay in the game.

"Is everything okay?" she asked softly, her eyes wide, lips parted. She stood in the doorway, framed by warm light.

Dillion stepped inside.

"Yeah," he said, voice hollow. "Sorry. You're the only person I thought to come to."

She closed the door gently. He looked at her—really looked. Her eyes had that soft glaze. Sadness? Or the pills she took for anxiety? The alcohol she sipped at parties?

She was beautiful and kind, but not Malia. She wouldn't understand. She had her own battles, her own demons. And this wasn't a story she could carry.

As they sat in her living room, a calmness washed over Dillion. He realized the reason he liked Rebecca wasn't just her beauty or presence, it was because he could be her confidant. Even though she seemed to have it all, she needed him just as much as he needed her. Still, he decided now wasn't the time to unload his burdens. He tucked his feelings behind thoughts of her, his new distraction.

"I was really worked up, but I'm better now," he said. "The drive here gave me time to decompress."

"Okay, well, if you want to talk, we can—"

"No, I'm fine."

"Don't bottle your feelings, Dillion."

Rebecca went upstairs. When she returned sometime later, she held a small clutch in her hand.

"Why'd you bring that down?" Dillion asked.

"I just thought you could use something to help you relax," she said. Then she paused, opened the clutch, and offered him one of her pills.

"I don't need that," Dillion said, eyeing the pill. "Do they really help with the pain? Or do they just numb you until it all comes crashing back, and you take more just to feel less again?"

Rebecca stared at him, then tilted her head back and took two pills herself. Her expression was steely, defiant. She didn't need his approval. This was her coping mechanism, her bunny. Dillion hoped one day she'd learn to let it go before it turned rabid.

"When did you start using them?" Dillion asked, trying to come from a place of understanding.

"I've been prescribed since high school. I always had test anxiety, performance stress. But I really started relying on them after freshman year—after I realized I couldn't play lacrosse anymore and came to terms with never living up to my dad's expectations. I guess I just started leaning on them more."

Dillion listened carefully. Beneath the polished exterior, Rebecca's voice was cracked with pain. It became clear—she, too, had lost her music.

As she spoke, tears welled in her eyes. Dillion had come here to decompress, to release stress, to rest his head on Rebecca. But the roles had reversed.

"Why do you feel like you need to meet your father's expectations?" Dillion asked.

"Why do you?" Rebecca shot back, catching him off guard. "Even though he's gone, you're still on a crusade to keep his ideals alive."

Dillion looked down at his feet. Her words struck a chord deep within him.

"You can't answer that, can you?" she continued. "You're not supposed to. But just imagine: what if your dad were still alive and active in your life? That's me."

He had never thought about it like that before. Was he really living out expectations that served neither him nor his father?

That night, Dillion and Rebecca talked for hours—about their childhoods, their pain, the moments that shaped them. Their lives had been so different, yet their stories were the same. Through their shared struggles, they forged a bond neither of them could explain, but both knew would be everlasting.

Chapter 15: The Clamp

In lacrosse, the clamp is a gritty, decisive move. A faceoff maneuver where a player pins down the ball with force and refuses to let go. Dillion is clamping down on his future, gripping his goals with relentless intensity. The ultimate goal is to gain possession and score.

Spring had arrived. The air carried the scent of blooming flowers and a crisp chill, hinting at the warmth of days to come. It was lacrosse season.

Georgetown was playing their best. After months of maturing and pushing each other, the team was one win away from securing a spot in the NCAA tournament. Dillion had worked his way up from second-line midfielder to starter. His speed, instinct, and knowledge of the game made all the difference. He had resisted being slotted in as a defender, believing that doing so would lock him into a role that didn't reflect his potential.

Now, that conviction was being rewarded. This was it. The moment he had been waiting for. Every sacrifice, every hour training, and every personal cost was all on the line. He had shut out everything else: his mother, Malia, the world he once knew. The only echoes of them came through in ignored texts: *"How are you?"* and *"Please call ... let's talk."* He dismissed them without a second thought. His world now consisted of school, lacrosse, and Rebecca.

It was game day. This game would determine their postseason fate. The air was sharp with cold; the grass was still damp with dew though it was nearly noon. The whistle blew. Sticks clashed. Feet pounded the turf. The game exploded with energy—it felt like an out-of-body experience. One minute they started; the next, they were leading by two goals in the second half. They just needed to lock in on defense.

When Dillion looked up, the clock had hit zero. They had won. Before he could even process it, his teammates swarmed the goalie. They had done it! The tournament awaited. This was the start of the real journey—win and you chase glory; lose and you go home.

Coach Yarling burst through the celebration, grabbing Dillion by the shoulders.

“Kid, I knew you were special,” he said, planting a kiss on Dillion’s head.

Gatorade and water rained down on him. He couldn’t tell if it was sweat or celebration, but it didn’t matter. This was the culmination of everything. The dream was alive.

He looked into the stands. No family. No Malia. Just teammates, roaring with triumph. This was his new life.

Rebecca jumped on him from behind.

“You guys were incredible! Wow!”

Dillion embraced her and lifted her off the ground. Emotions surged through him. He walked off the field, surrounded by the chaos of victory, his focus already shifting forward.

In the locker room, the team erupted in celebration. Coach praised everyone, but Dillion sat against his locker, soaking it all in. It felt good, but he knew this was only the beginning. The hardest battles were still ahead.

That night, drained from the game, Dillion returned to his room. Ice bags wrapped around his legs, books scattered across his bed, notebooks stacked on his nightstand. Finals loomed, and the strain of late-season play was catching up with his academics. He needed to catch up—fast.

Isaac burst through the door.

“Dude! You’re actually here! You’ve been at Rebecca’s so much, I forgot I had a roommate.”

Dillion sighed, placing his book down. No point trying to study now.

“I figured you’d be out partying. Thought I could study in peace.”

“You’re doing schoolwork? Man, you’re about to win a national championship!”

“Yeah, well, that’s why they call us student-athletes, Isaac.”

“What do you have to do?”

“Term papers. The usual.”

“How about I help you out? I’ll handle your essays—you just owe me one.”

“What do you mean?”

“I have a friend who can hook you up. You know what I mean? You think all the other athletes on campus do their own work?”

“Yeah, I do. I’ve always done my own work. It’s stressful, but I’ll get it done.”

“Look, this is a big deal—for the school and for you. It’s not a crime to get a little help. You're about to make history. You've already done the hard part. Everyone needs a boost now and then. Just give me the outlines and books. I got you. Don’t worry.”

“I don’t know, Isaac. This doesn’t feel right.”

"Don't you want to win? This is monumental. A freshman leading the team to a potential championship? You've got three more years to stress over school. Let this be my favor to you. Just win the title and remember the little guy who had your back."

Dillion's body ached. His head was numb. Maybe he was dehydrated. The idea of not having to worry about school started to sound comforting.

"It's all good," Isaac said, seeing him waver.

Dillion sat, sore and mentally exhausted. He opened his mouth to speak, but his phone buzzed. *Malia.* What could she want right now? He silenced the phone.

"Okay," Dillion finally said. "I'm trusting you. You sure you can handle it?"

"Trust me, bro."

"I don't want this biting me later. Keep this between us."

"Scout's honor."

Chapter 16: Rusty Gate

In lacrosse, the "rusty gate" is an unconventional, risky check—a flashy defensive move that can backfire if mistimed. That's exactly what this championship game feels like for Dillion: an unpredictable battle where instinct meets pressure and one wrong move can cost it all. As his team takes the field against the powerhouse Hopkins squad, Dillion is targeted, rattled, and forced to confront not only his opponents but his own ghosts from last season's collapse. But as chaos swirls and doubts creep in, he rediscovers the deeper meaning of the game: its roots in unity, humility, and purpose.

Coach strode into the locker room, brim of his hat bent low, hand running through his hair. The team pulled out their earbuds, turning to him like sunflowers chasing the sun at high noon.

"Here we are, fellas. This is what you worked for. This is why you picked up a stick in the first place. To control your fate.

While little Timmy was nestled in bed, you were grinding—running drills, lifting weights. The pain, the sacrifice—this is what it's about. You only get a few truly special moments in life. People say it's the birth of your child or getting married, but I wonder if those people ever had the chance to win an NCAA lacrosse championship. If they did, I bet they didn't win it. Because this … this is the pinnacle.

I'm not giving you a rah-rah speech. It's time to put your hard hat on. Your stick is your shovel. Your work ethic is your lunch pail. Let's go to work."

The team let out a guttural roar. This was it—the Big Show.

Dillion stood, eyes scanning the room, feeling the moment stretch and warp around him. Walking through the tunnel, he saw the glimmer of sunlight reflecting off the turf. The crowd's hum grew louder with each step. Officials dotted the field, preparing for the opening ceremony.

He gripped his stick tight, punching the mesh inside the head. Firm. Just the way he liked it.

It was warm out. Memorial Day. Championship Day, as always.

The captains moved down the line, slapping helmets, speaking affirmations. Lathan stopped in front of Dillion.

"Brother, this is your time. We need you. You got us here—finish it."

Lathan's eyes burned. This was his last ride. His final shot. And everyone knew it: Dillion was the heart. The engine of this machine.

An event coordinator jogged up.

"Fireworks are your cue. That's when you take the field!"

And just as fast, he disappeared.

Then came the boom. Fireworks cracked. The crowd erupted. The team charged out together. The anthem played. Starters took their positions. Goalie met goalie. Game time.

Dillion lined up for the face-off. His opponent wore baby blue and white. Johns Hopkins, the team Dillion grew up idolizing. He'd spent countless Saturdays there with his dad, watching games and eating food truck tacos on the track. This was sacred ground.

He stared into the opposing player's eyes. Focus. He could feel it. The player switched to a motorcycle grip—something they hadn't shown on film. The whistle blew.

Dillion clamped down. Smooth. Crisp. The ball popped into his pocket. Adrenaline surged—crack!—a stick to his arm. He switched hands. Wham! He was on the ground. The hit came fast—too fast. They weren't playing like they did on film.

Dillion rolled to his knees, watching the other team storm the field. The crowd erupted. 1–0.

He jogged to the sideline, lungs burning. Coach rushed to him.

"You okay?"

"Yeah … I didn't expect that."

"None of us did. Catch your breath. We need you."

Dillion sprayed water over his helmet, watching formations. Same playbook. Maybe it was a fluke.

He got the signal. Subbed back in. Another goal. 2–0.

Back at the X, a new opponent—same grip. Whistle. Dillion won the clamp again, but slowed, scanning the field.

Crack! A body check slammed into his chest like a freight train. No flag.

He gasped on the ground. Are they trying to take me out? Coach called him off. They locked eyes. They both knew what was happening.

Dillion dumped water over his head, trying to cool his frustration. This was different. They were in his head.

He sat on the bench, mind racing. He knew lacrosse wasn't just a game—it was games within a game. Strategy, intensity, endurance ... and chess. All season, he was the X-factor. No one had footage. No one had answers. Now, they did.

He looked at the Hopkins bench. He'd played there in high school. Maybe they remembered. Maybe they studied his every move since then.

He subbed in again—and watched two long poles sub in with him. That's when he knew: their best offense was defense; they were targeting him.

The next pass flew overhead—he hadn't even seen it. He was too focused on them. Coach pulled him.

"Dillion, don't let them get in your head."

But they already had. He'd been here before last year. A lost championship. A heavy burden. And the memories came flooding back—every mistake, every doubt, every second of pain.

This is a powerful continuation, raw and emotional, with a clear arc of transformation for Dillion and his team. He had to change his focus.

Dillion looked at his teammates—really looked. He thought about how they had played all season, the chemistry they'd built, the battles they'd fought. This wasn't last year's team. This wasn't the same Dillion either.

In the middle of the frustration and exhaustion, he forced himself to examine the game's first half—not as a victim, but as a creator. What details had he missed before? What lessons had been buried in last year's pain? He had to transform the scars of the past into the fire that would guide the present.

They had to adjust. Every one of them had gifts. But gifts without harmony meant nothing. This game wasn't about him. Not anymore.

He thought of the Creator. The game's roots. The sacredness of lacrosse. This was a game of inclusion, unity, respect. It demanded selflessness. The Creator wouldn't want one man to carry the burden alone; the game was about the collective. One soul. Many parts.

The buzzer blared. They were down. Dillion raised his head and walked with the team into the locker room. Coach peeled off his hat, exposing sweaty hair. He wiped the sweat from his brow and paced for a moment, then turned.

"Look, guys," Coach began, voice raw. "I don't know what else to say at this point in the season. They're giving us matchup problems, and to be honest, it looks like they want it more. Some of you are just happy to be here. Happy to be in the conversation. But I'm not. I'm here to win."

He paused, eyes sharp.

"The world's about solving problems. The ones who do that the best? They win. Period."

Dillion stepped forward. He never spoke in team huddles—not like this. But something inside him wouldn't let him stay silent.

"We have to change the way we *think* about this game," he said. "If we change how we *see* it, the game itself will change."

The locker room stilled.

"We're acting like we don't deserve to win. Like we have to fight for it. But we've already won. We made it here together. This is ours if we believe it.

We have to be one soul. Many pieces. One thought. One goal.

Close your eyes for a second. Envision it—each of us doing our job, making the big play, lifting each other up. See the guy next to you succeeding. See it."

One by one, the players closed their eyes.

Dillion kept going. The words came naturally now, like they'd always been inside him.

"See the little things—us talking, moving together, trusting each other. See Coach holding the trophy. See yourself in the championship shirt, the hat. See the crowd, the celebration.

What we need isn't new plays. We don't need X's and O's right now. We need to change our minds. That's what changes the game."

They locked arms. The room shifted. You could feel it—the belief. Not just hope. *Knowing.*

When the second half began, something was different. Dillion won the next faceoff. The ball moved fluidly, everyone touched it. They played calmly and confidently, together. They played free. They weren't fighting the game; they were flowing with it.

With 60 seconds left, the score was tied. Hopkins had just scored. The stadium was electric. But Dillion didn't panic. He walked to the X. His hands were sore, but he had no other option. This was the moment.

The whistle blew. He exploded forward, wrenching his stick and body into the ground. The ball jammed between the two crosses. Locked. Neither moved.

Then, pop! The ball launched into the air. They both chased it like kids scrambling for the last Easter egg. They collided, swinging and swiping.

Hopkins scooped the ball. Dillion didn't hesitate. He sprinted after his opponent and laid his shoulder square into the attacker's chest like a linebacker. They both crashed to the turf.

Dillion blinked, dazed. Then, shouts. Movement.

Who had the ball? He scrambled up and saw it—Georgetown! His team!

He took off, trailing the play. The defense was unsettled. Lathan dodged, took a hit, but passed just in time.

The attackman caught it, faked a shot. A defender lunged, but the angle wasn't right.

The ball flew back toward Dillion. He wasn't ready. He'd expected a shot, not a pass.

No, he thought. But his body reacted. He reached high, snagging the pass over his left shoulder.

Four seconds left. Two steps. He unleashed the shot with everything he had. The goalie split—desperate. But too late. The net rippled. Game over.

Georgetown were national champions.

For a moment, Dillion just stood there, stunned. Then chaos erupted—helmets and sticks in the air, players swarming like wild men. Dillion blinked. Was it real?

His teammates tackled him, laughing, crying, screaming. He scanned the stands, his school's section a frenzy of celebration.

But something tugged at his heart. His mother. Malia. Even his dad. He wished they could've seen this … felt this. He felt victory, but also a strange emptiness.

Then he saw them—Rebecca, Isaac, and their families, rushing down the steps. The past was the past. This... this was his future.

The team returned to campus as heroes. The celebration was unlike anything the school had ever seen. But even champions had classes to attend.

Dillion walked through the halls in his championship gear, his shirt still smelling faintly of turf and sweat and glory. He felt invincible. The world had changed.

He stepped into his first class of the week, still riding the high. Students offered fist bumps and congratulations. He smiled, nodded, basked in the moment.

The professor droned on, his voice a muffled blur, like the adults in the Peanuts cartoons Dillion's mom used to mention.

Class neared its end.

"Dillion," the professor said, suddenly clear, "could I speak with you after class?"

Dillion nodded, heart light. Maybe he wanted a picture. Maybe he was a fan.

He gathered his things, waved at a few classmates, then approached.

"Yes, sir?" Dillion said, trying to sound humble.

The professor packed up his laptop, closing his leather attaché.

"Do you have a few minutes? Let's talk in my office. It's just down the hall."

Dillion was a bit put off but figured the teacher wanted to be discreet, with students streaming in for the next lecture. They walked down the crowded hallway in silence—lacrosse players signing autographs, fans snapping pictures, the energy still buzzing from the championship win. At the end of the hall, the teacher opened the door to his office.

"Have a seat, Dillion," he said, closing the door behind them.

Dillion sat, immediately noticing a change in tone. Something felt off.

"What's up, Teach? Everything okay?" he asked, trying to sound casual, though unease crept into his voice.

"I'm afraid it's not," the teacher said, reaching toward a stack of papers on his desk. "We have a serious issue."

The hairs on the back of Dillion's neck stood up. His stomach twisted. He braced himself.

"This department has been alerted," the teacher continued, "that a student—or possibly multiple students—have not been honest in their academic work."

"I'm ... confused, sir." Dillion leaned forward, squinting at the paper the teacher held.

It had his name in the corner: *Dillion Frank.* But the rest looked unfamiliar.

"This paper was flagged," the teacher said. "It's shown up in our system before. Multiple times, actually. Identical copies."

Dillion's heart plummeted. His first thought was *Isaac.* He *promised.*

"It's a good piece of work," the teacher added. "But it's not original. And that's a violation of academic integrity."

Dillion slumped in his chair. There was no play to run, no defense to call. Just silence and shame.

"The administration has been notified. The policy is strict. They're moving to dismiss you and vacate this semester. All your classes are under review. I wanted to let you know before it hits officially."

Dillion was speechless. His voice caught in his throat. How had he let this happen? A moment of weakness—just one—and now it threatened to erase everything he'd worked for. The championship, the brotherhood, the future.

He walked out of the office a different man than the one who entered. Defeated. Numb.

Back in his dorm, he found Isaac lying on the bed, headphones on, oblivious. Dillion stormed over and yanked them off.

"Did you know about this?" Dillion threw the paper at him.

Isaac sat up, startled, catching the sheet midair. He scanned it.

"Looks like the paper I submitted for you," he said slowly.

"Well, it's not mine. It's someone else's. They think I'm a fraud, Isaac! I trusted you!" Dillion's voice cracked with anger and disbelief.

"Shit," Isaac whispered, running his hands through his hair. "Shit."

Dillion paced the room, his mind spinning.

"Coach. Maybe Coach can help," he muttered, bolting out of the dorm without another word.

He sprinted to the athletic complex, the weight of the moment pulling on every step. He reached Coach's office and saw him through the glass—tired, slumped, his back turned.

Dillion knocked. Coach turned in his chair, placed his glasses on, and gestured for him to come in.

"Sit down," he said with a sigh.

"You already know, huh?" Dillion asked.

"Yeah. Wish they'd handled it differently. We've got a meeting tomorrow. They're coming down hard. They want to make an example out of you so it doesn't happen again. That way we don't risk losing the championship."

"Is there anything the program can do?" Dillion asked, desperate. "I can't get dismissed, Coach."

"We've been in talks all morning. But I think we're going to have to step back. It's for the team, Dillion. The school's handling it now."

Dillion's eyes welled up. "I gave everything to this team..."

"I know," Coach said gently. "But this? You've got to own it."

Tears streamed down Dillion's face. Just hours ago, he was a hero. Now, he felt abandoned. His world, the world he'd fought for, was unraveling.

He wanted to blame Isaac, the coaches, the teachers, his father for pushing him here. But deep down, he knew—it had been his choice. And the consequences were his alone.

He wiped his face, stood, and turned to leave.

Was there anyone left?

He left the coach's office without another word and walked back to his dorm. He changed into his training gear. He had to run—*that* was something he still understood.

Dillion hit the pavement. His thoughts were loud, his emotions even louder, but his feet knew the rhythm. As he ran—up hills, over cracked sidewalks, up concrete steps—the weight of it all began to burn off, bit by bit. The anxiety slowly peeled away with every drop of sweat.

He didn't know how far he'd gone. He just knew he had to run until the noise in his head quieted.

By the time he got back to his dorm, he was drenched. Isaac was gone—not that Dillion was ready to face him anyway. He stepped into the shower and let the hot water rinse off the sweat, the shame, and the regret, if only for a moment. He dressed in fresh clothes, pulling on his most comfortable cotton socks, the small comfort grounding him just enough to take the next step.

Rebecca.

He left with his head low, thoughts still churning. It all still felt unreal—like someone else's life unraveling in his hands.

When he reached Rebecca's house and raised his hand to knock, the door flew open.

"Where have you *been*?" Rebecca said, frustration heavy in her voice.

"Issac told me everything. I've been trying to call you like crazy."

Dillion blinked. His phone. He had no idea where it was—maybe in his locker, maybe on the field. It didn't matter.

He opened his mouth to speak, but no words came before Rebecca pulled him inside.

"My dad called me too looking for you. Isaac told his father what happened, and *he* called my dad to see what we could do."

"I'm just ... disappointed in myself," Dillion muttered, tears rising again, uninvited.

Rebecca disappeared into the kitchen and returned moments later with a large glass of water and a charcuterie board.

"Well, my father wants to meet with you. Tomorrow at 4 p.m. at the Georgetown Club. He's not happy with Isaac or any of this, but I think he can help you."

"The Georgetown Club?" Dillion asked, stuffing a piece of salami and cheese into his mouth—his first food of the day.

"It's a members-only club up on Wisconsin Avenue. I'll go with you. He holds all his business meetings there. When I was a little girl, I used to think it was a secret clubhouse or something. I even imagined having my wedding reception there ... but anyway, that's not important."

"You know what he wants to talk about?"

"No. He didn't say on the phone. But he wouldn't ask to meet with you *there* if it wasn't something serious. Some kind of guidance, maybe. My dad doesn't do casual."

"Damn Isaac," she muttered. "He's always getting himself—and everyone around him—into messes."

Rebecca reached into her blouse pocket and pulled out her familiar pill bottle. She placed one on her tongue and chased it with a sip from Dillion's water.

Dillion frowned. "Why *you* stressed?"

She exhaled. "Because this whole thing is just wrong. Isaac brought my family into it, now my dad's getting involved ... and I don't know. I feel responsible too."

"You didn't do anything."

Rebecca hesitated. Then, quietly: "It was my paper he used."

Dillion froze as he was halfway through another piece of cheese. He stared at her.

"What?"

She looked away.

"He used *my* paper."

Silence hung in the air like fog.

Did she know more than she was letting on? Was there even more to uncover?

Acknowledgements

After spending several years writing this book, I can honestly say this is the hardest page to write. There are so many people who helped shape the creation of this work, and if I happen to forget anyone, please forgive me. Blame my head, not my heart.
First, I want to thank our Creator, who gave me divine inspiration and the strength to create.

To my mother, Wanda Randolph. You've carried me far beyond the nine months, and you have always been my true rock.

To my father, Wilmont Randolph. As I've become a man, I respect you more each day. For a man to raise a son who does not share your last name or your DNA, you have given me so much. I see you now more clearly, and I thank you.

To my womb mate, Delmar Randolph. Thank you for always being by my side.

To my wife, Stephanie Frank. You have shared life with me, walked through trials and triumphs, and supported me through it all. Thank you for your love and your strength.

To my bonus mother, Gertrude Frank, and my sisters, Stephanie and Nicole. You constantly remind me who I am every time I see myself reflected in you. Your presence has grounded me.

To my sons, Knighten and Truce Frank. You are my muses, the heartbeat of this story, and the reason I strive to build and leave behind something meaningful. Thank you for inspiring me every day.

Special thanks to Tia Thompson, who helped me shape the early stages of this book, and to Julie Allen and Che Allen, who challenged my thinking and pushed me to go deeper into the subject matter.

To Anthony Commodore, my mentor, and Ayanna Moo-Young. You saw an uncut diamond and understood its value before I did. You helped refine my project and bring it into its fullest form.

To the coaches who showed me the right way and believed in my athletic potential, George Drummy and Johnny Watson. You opened doors for me and placed me in spaces I once only dreamed about.

To the organizations that trusted me to lead and coach young men, thank you:
Aberdeen Jr Lacrosse and Chris Allen
Ground Control Lacrosse and Brian Outten
Forest Hill Lacrosse
Patterson Mill High School
Emmorton Rec Football and Tom Rohal
Bel Air Terps Football and Mike Moore
USA Lacrosse

To the organizations that gave my sons a home in the sport we love:
The John Carroll School
Crabs Lacrosse Club
Bel Air Blue Claws
North Stars Lacrosse

A special shout out to Sammi Curreri, my guy and a true staple in Baltimore lacrosse. Thank you for always being present and showing love.

In loving memory of John Frank and Barbra Marsh. Your presence is still felt, your impact still alive. This work carries part of you with it.

To everyone who played a part in this journey, whether named here or held in my heart, thank you. This book may have my name on it, but it carries the love, lessons, and energy of so many others.

With love and gratitude.

About the Author

Derrick J. Frank is the Chief Executive Officer of Knighten Truce LLC, a Maryland-based media company creating bold and innovative content for the modern world. With nearly twenty years of experience working in the nation's capital, Derrick brings a unique blend of creative vision, leadership, and community-driven purpose to everything he does.

He began his post-secondary academic journey at Shepherd University and earned a degree from Frostburg State University. He later completed a certificate program at Harvard Business School, deepening his expertise in business strategy and leadership.

Outside of his professional life, Derrick is a devoted husband, father and longtime youth coach. He has led teams in football and basketball, but his greatest passion is lacrosse, a sport he has coached at recreational, club, and high school levels. Whether mentoring young athletes or writing stories that challenge and uplift, Derrick is driven by a single mission: to inspire the next generation to dream big, stay grounded, and lead with heart.